THE PONY DETECTIVES

Puzzle

the Runaway Pony

First published in the UK in 2012 by Templar Publishing,

an imprint of The Templar Company Limited,

The Granary, North Street, Dorking, Surrey, RH4 1DN, UK

www.templarco.co.uk

Copyright © 2012 by Belinda Rapley

Cover design by Will Steele

Illustrations by Debbie Clark and Dave Shephard

Cover photo by Samantha Lamb

First edition second impression

ISBN 978-1-84877-835-1

Printed and bound by CPI Group (UK) Ltd, Croydon, CR0 4YY

THE PONY DETECTIVES

Book Three

Puzzle

the Runaway Pony

by Belinda Rapley

templar

For Joanne & Andy and Jonathan & Hayley

Rosie and Dancer

Mia and Wish

Alice and Scout

Charlie and Pirate

Chapter One

THE ponies kept their heads down to avoid the buffeting wind as they clopped along the lane. Rosie felt a large raindrop hit the back of her neck and trickle down beneath her jacket. With a shudder she looked up at the inky-grey clouds hanging in the early October skies. There wasn't a break in sight. Thunder rumbled in the distance.

"Hands up if you think we should abandon this mission and go home," Rosie said grumpily, as she felt another fat wet drop, then another. Her strawberry roan mare, Dancer, was already growing her winter coat, turning her body whiter while her head, lower legs, mane and tail stayed chestnut. But even with her thicker coat, Dancer still looked as miserable and cold as Rosie felt, her ears back, her forelock stuck to the white blaze on her face from an earlier downpour. "I said this was a bad idea from the start. We're about to get seriously drenched again. I can *smell* the rain coming..."

It had rained almost non-stop for a week, scuppering any plans for a long ride at the start of the weekend. Instead, they'd had to spend all day Saturday grooming their ponies and hanging around in the hay barn reading *Pony Mad*. It was still raining on Sunday morning when they arrived at Blackberry Farm, but Charlie insisted that they'd have to hack out, no matter what, after the ponies had been fed.

"Charlie's right," Mia had agreed. "If we wait for the rain to stop completely we might end up not riding all weekend."

"And we're not exactly going to uncover any new mysteries hanging about at the yard all day," Charlie added. "We need to go for lots of hacks to find them!"

At the start of the summer, Charlie, Mia, Rosie and Alice had decided to call themselves the Pony Detectives, after tracking down Moonlight, a top local show jumper who'd been stolen just before the Fratton show. They'd taken on their second case at the end of the summer holidays, when Alice's pony Scout was unexpectedly put up for sale by his shady owner. With help from the RSPCA, they'd worked quickly to unravel the mystery surrounding Scout's past to save him from being sold. But that felt like ages ago now, and they hadn't had a single mystery to solve since.

Rosie was as desperate as the others to discover a new case, but she was still less than impressed with the prospect of riding out that day. She'd already argued that they should postpone it until the rain stopped because she had 'unreliable, leaky clothing', but the others were having none of it.

"Let's take a vote, then," Rosie had suggested, her pale blue eyes and English rose complexion framed by her long, straw-coloured flyaway hair.

"Who thinks we should go and get soaked – which, I might say, Dancer detests – and who thinks we should stay here in the barn where there is cake and hot chocolate available? Oh, that and the opportunity to *stay dry!*"

"Erm, I don't really mind either way..." Alice said, being indecisive. Her shoulder-length mousy-brown hair fell forward as she buried her face in Beanie, Rosie's Jack Russell dog, to avoid the dark stare Rosie was giving her from across the tack room.

On the one hand, Alice knew that Scout, the dappled grey pony she now had on permanent loan from the RSPCA, was a hardy Connemara cross and didn't mind the wet weather. On the other hand, her ancient jacket and baggy jods weren't exactly warm. But then she knew Scout was much happier getting out and being ridden than being cooped up all day.

"Well, I definitely want to go for a ride, whatever the weather," Charlie added, shoving her hat over her dark elfin-style hair, her green eyes cheerful as she grabbed her tack. "And so will Pirate."

"Rain won't stop me riding either, so you're outvoted, Rosie." Mia smiled. Her part-bred arab, Wish Me Luck, had such thin skin beneath her silky palomino-coloured coat that Mia's parents had splashed out on every possible bit of warm, waterproof gear for her. And for Mia herself. "Come on, let's go!"

Once they were out riding the rain had stopped for a bit, but now the sky was darkening rapidly again and raindrops were starting to fall.

"We're almost there, Rosie," Charlie reassured her as she led the way on her small native pony, Pirate. He was at the front of the line of four, his small stubby ears pricked, bright and eager to keep going, and not even noticing any rain. His bushy black mane and forelock kept most of his chunky neck and mischievous face dry as they followed the route Charlie had mapped out in the hay barn

the day before. "Anyway, this is an adventure –
we've never ridden out here. It's exciting!"

Rosie scowled as a gust of wind whipped off
her riding silk and she almost fell out of the saddle
leaning to pull it from a nearby branch. She
tugged it wonkily back over her skull cap,
grumbling to herself.

As Alice giggled at her friend, the faint beat of
fast, rhythmic trotting hooves sounded on the
lane behind them, quickly growing louder. The
girls' ponies pricked their ears, turning their heads
as three smartly turned-out ponies approached
from behind. Their riders pulled the ponies out
wide to overtake. Rosie, Alice and Charlie all
looked across and gave friendly smiles.

"Hi there," Mia called out.

The two girls trotting together in front
ignored Mia's greeting completely, but one of
them, riding a chestnut, then nodded towards
Charlie and smirked.

"How ridiculous – look! That girl must have

got on the wrong pony when she left the yard this morning," she said, purposely loud. "Or maybe her pony just shrank in the rain!"

The girl on a fine dun next to her looked at Pirate then burst out laughing.

"You're so right, Sasha," she snorted. "She's way too tall for that poor pony. I'm surprised he can move!"

Charlie went pink as she realised that they were talking about her, her smile fading quickly. She'd grown a lot taller recently and her stirrups had started to dangle well below her pony's elbows. She was light, though, and she knew that Pirate was strong and stocky enough to carry her.

A red-headed girl, who was trotting behind on a pretty skewbald pony, half-smiled at the Pony Detectives apologetically. The girl called Sasha spotted this, and tutted.

"If you don't find me funny, Bex," she said, scowling, "you could always leave the CM club, you know."

Bex looked as if she was going to reply, then thought better of it. She dropped her head as the other two smirked again before all three disappeared around a bend in the lane ahead.

"Great!" Rosie said indignantly. "Now we're being attacked by random riders as well as the rain!"

"Ignore them, Charlie," Alice said, jogging Scout up to walk alongside Pirate. "They're just being mean."

Charlie nodded, smiling a bit too brightly as she patted Pirate's thick neck. She'd had her pony for years, and they knew each other so well that she could anticipate his every move, sitting effortlessly to his excited bucks and his impatient spins as they charged about the countryside. She just had to think something and he'd do it. And Pirate was a daredevil: he'd tackle absolutely anything with gusto. No jump was too high, and that suited her completely.

When she'd first got him he'd been too big, and she'd had to loop her stirrup leathers to get them short enough. He'd been pretty wild and she'd fallen off a lot, but as they'd grown up together Charlie had become more confident and now they were inseparable, best friends. She'd always thought that outgrowing Pirate would be something to worry about in the future. Only, that girl's comments had made her realise with a sudden jolt like being hit by lightning, leaving her insides fizzing, that the future was already here. Everything was suddenly, horribly real and she knew, deep down, that she couldn't pretend it wasn't happening, not even for just a little bit longer.

"Alice is right, Charlie," Mia added, noticing her thoughtful, unusual silence. "Their manners are clearly nowhere near as lovely as their ponies."

Charlie shrugged breezily, as if she wasn't bothered.

"I guess. Anyway, looks like we're here," she said, quickly changing the subject and firmly pushing all thoughts about Pirate and their future together from her mind. "I reckon that must be Compton Manor!"

"Ooh, yes!" Mia squinted through the drizzle to a smart, open gate further along the tree-lined lane. "There it is!"

"Finally!" Rosie said melodramatically.

They rode to the open gate and pulled the ponies up. There, set back from the grand, sweeping drive, sat the Manor House. In front of it was the brand new competition and livery yard which had opened six months ago. It cost a fortune to stable a horse there, but according to its website it had first-class facilities, with one outdoor and two indoor schools, a jumping paddock, a cross-country course and vast American barns big enough to stable forty horses.

"Apparently one barn's kept *exclusively* for junior riders of sixteen years and under," Mia pointed out as they looked at the imposing grounds ahead of them. "They run the barn themselves too. I bet it's amazing!"

"It sounds just like Blackberry Farm, if you ask me," Rosie replied, looking slightly disgruntled. The four girls kept their ponies at the Farm, which Rosie's parents had inherited from an ancient aunt. It had a cottage, where Rosie lived with her artist mum and her farmer dad and older brother, Will. As well as the cottage there were acres of turnout and a small, eight-box yard. The girls were in charge, after Mrs Honeycott, Rosie's mum, said that they could all keep their ponies there, but only on the condition that they were responsible for looking after everything themselves. "After all, we're all under sixteen and we run our yard, too; I don't see the difference."

Mia raised her eyebrows as she looked over at Rosie, thinking that the ramshackle yard could hardly be compared to the Manor. They'd been waiting for a show to be held there so they could get a proper look round. That moment had almost arrived: in a fortnight's time Compton Manor was holding its first indoor jumping competition.

"Okay, well, we've seen it now and we know how to get here for the show," Rosie said, trying to bury her head in the neck of her jacket. She was the least excited of the four about getting to peek inside the exclusive yard, given that Dancer wasn't much of a jumper and she was the least competitive of her friends. "So can we please go home? I'm seriously about to pass out from hypothermia."

Alice shivered. "Rosie's got a point," she said. "I'd so *love* to be tucked up in the barn right now with a delicious hot chocolate to warm my hands on. My fingers are almost numb!"

At that moment Dancer spun her bottom round neatly so that her tail faced the sharp wind. As another gust billowed up, she tucked her tail in pointedly.

"See, even Dancer's turned for home," Rosie added with an exaggerated shiver. "She's normally *so* enthusiastic when I ride her that this *must* be a sign that we should head back."

Charlie and Alice giggled at Rosie, who smiled sheepishly. They all knew how lazy and sluggish Dancer was, even on her 'energetic' days.

"Come on – now we're here, lets pick up some entry forms for the show," Mia said, tucked up snugly in her fleece-lined waterproof jacket and matching trousers. "That way we can have a quick nose around at the same time..."

They followed Mia, nudging each other as they rode up a wide driveway between immaculately manicured lawns. They dismounted and walked into the yard, suddenly feeling scruffy and mud-splattered among all the neat perfection that surrounded them. Mia couldn't help but be impressed by the smart barns, with their rows of brand-new stables.

To the left stood an outdoor school, which had lots of brightly coloured jumps set up inside it. They watched for a moment as a young rider schooled his cobby cremello pony quietly between them. Then the three girls who'd trotted past them earlier emerged from the smallest barn. Sasha, the girl who'd made the mean comment about Charlie, was still riding her chestnut pony, but the other two were following on foot as they headed towards the outdoor school. When Sasha caught sight of the boy already in there, she smirked.

"Tom, are you stupid?" she called out. The girl next to her giggled. Bex stood a step back from them, looking slightly awkward. "This is the *jumping* school, and you're not jumping."

"I'm just warming Casper up," Tom explained as he cantered past. "I'll be jumping him in a bit."

"Well 'in a bit' isn't now," Sasha pointed out, "and I'm ready to jump The Colonel, so you'll just have to find somewhere else to school Casper."

"Can't," Tom said, circling. "The indoor schools are being used by the seniors – I've already checked. Anyway, why can't we both ride in here? It's big enough."

"Because, Tom," Sasha called, glancing over to

the Pony Detectives, "I have a special project on and I need the whole space. And you shouldn't be arguing with me anyway. *I* run the Junior yard so what I say goes. Got it?"

Tom hesitated for a second, then with a sigh, brought Casper to a walk.

"Whatever," he said, opening the gate.

"Good," Sasha said, smiling sweetly for a second before adding, "although for taking ages, I'm putting you on muck-heap duty next week."

Tom fumed as he walked his pony out. As he passed by, Casper left a trail of sand from the school behind him.

"You'd better make sure you come back and sweep that up," Sasha said, "or I'll report you to Mum."

Sasha had already clocked Mia, Alice, Rosie and Charlie, and now she kicked her chestnut into a walk and headed over to them.

"Sorry about that," she smiled, although Charlie couldn't help wondering if the whole episode had been for their benefit, "but you know what it's like. When you're in charge you have to remind everyone who's boss every now and again."

Mia was convinced that Sasha's 'every now and again' really meant 'all the time'. To get that good at being mean took practice.

"Anyway, you're the ones from the ride just now, aren't you?" Sasha said. "So, how can I help? The Junior yard's full and the waiting list is huge. And I'm really picky about who I let join it, too."

Sasha looked them all up and down, pointedly.

"Oh, we only came for some entry forms for the show," Mia said, trying to keep the irritation out of her voice.

"Which classes are you entering?" Sasha asked, gathering up her chestnut's reins. Alice felt sorry for him – judging by the sweat on his flanks he'd already done more than enough without being jumped too. "*I've* designed the course for the Junior Trophy myself."

"With your mum's help," Bex pointed out. Sasha scowled at her.

"She approved my design," Sasha said coolly, "but *I* was the genius behind it."

"Whatever, there's no point in any of you entering the Trophy," the other girl, who had short blonde hair, said quickly. "Sasha and The Colonel are unbeatable."

"The forms are in the office if you *do* want to bother," Sasha said. "But Jade's right. The Colonel's a jumping machine. Anyway, I can't sit around here all day – I've got to get some practice in."

"Not that you need any," Bex said, forcing a smile.

"Don't be a creep, Bex," Jade tutted.

"If you're not careful, Bex," Sasha sighed as they turned back to the school, "I *will* throw you out of the CM club, just because you're annoying me. Now, change those fences round. You know where."

"That's the second time Sasha's mentioned the

CM club," Alice said, looking over to the school. "I wonder what it is?"

"I don't know, but if Sasha's in it," Rosie muttered, "I doubt it's very nice."

The Pony Detectives watched Bex and Jade altering the poles while Sasha pointed and barked orders. Then she cantered round on her pony before starting to jump the huge fences. The Colonel was slick over them, but as he jumped he swished his tail round and round, his ears back.

"He doesn't exactly look happy, does he?" Rosie commented quietly as they stood and watched for a moment.

"A bit like everyone else around here," Charlie said, frowning.

She took Wish's reins as Mia ducked into the office to find the entry forms. Tom had quickly put Casper away and followed Mia in there, looking red and flustered.

"Mrs Compton," he said as the woman behind the desk pointed out the forms to Mia. Mia lingered, slowly counting out her handful of forms so that she could eavesdrop. "I want to report a problem..."

"Yes, well, Tom, you're from the Under 16s yard, aren't you?" Mrs Compton said, glancing up at him then back down to her paperwork. "So you know how this all works. You have to talk to my daughter Sasha if you have any problems. She's in charge of your yard."

"But it's *about* Sasha…" Tom started, sounding frustrated.

"Like I said, all complaints go through Sasha," Mrs Compton cut in, peering over her half-moon glasses. "If she can't deal with it, then she'll talk to me. Now, I'm very busy."

Mrs Compton waved her hand, dismissing Tom in an instant. He rolled his eyes as he turned and stomped out. Mia followed him, thinking that however nice Compton Manor looked from the outside, it was the least friendly yard she'd ever set foot on.

Chapter Two

"I CAN'T believe I ever thought for a second about stabling Wish there!" Mia said as they rode back up the drive and out onto the lane.

"What?!" Rosie asked, alarmed. "Did you really want to leave Blackberry Farm?"

"No, of course not, not seriously," Mia laughed, "but it did look totally amazing when I saw it online."

"Exactly – I mean, everything looks perfect, and you'd think anyone would be over the moon about being there," Alice agreed, "but instead they're all miserable."

"I guess all you need is the people in charge to be horrible," Charlie said, "and it has a knock-on effect on everyone."

"Just like Blackberry Farm," Alice joked.

"That's it, Alice Hathaway, you're out!" Rosie laughed. "Right, let's go home!"

As they all turned their ponies onto the lane, heading back in the direction they'd come from, Charlie jogged Pirate to the lead.

"If we turn down this little side lane, rather than carrying on along the main one," she said, pulling the scrap of paper on which she'd drawn the route to Compton Manor from her pocket, "we should find a bridleway a bit further up on the left, leading into the woods. It looks like a good one, so we can have a really fast canter to warm up! It's just up here, I think…"

At that moment a gust of wind flapped the paper out of Charlie's gloved hand, spooking Pirate, who danced sideways in a clatter of hooves. They all watched as it fluttered furiously out of sight.

"Not to worry," Charlie said uncertainly as her teeth started to chatter. "I'm sure I can remember the way."

Silently, the four turned their ponies down the narrow, dank lane. The ponies' hooves were the only noise as they clopped alongside the thick woods which lined the lane to their left. Rosie pointed out that the raindrops had started to fall more frequently, specifically the ones going down her neck. Charlie saw a narrow gap into the woods and frowned.

"I reckon this must be the path," she announced, peering through the gloomy archway of trees. "If we gallop along this bit, we might even make it home before the rain really comes down."

At first the bridleway looked quite promising and they managed to have a few strides of canter before trotting for quite a way. Lots of small paths criss-crossed the path they were riding along and Charlie peered down each one. She couldn't remember if they were meant to turn off, so she decided to keep going on the winding path, dodging between trees and bushes. But they soon faltered to a walk.

"Are you sure this is right?" Alice asked as another narrow path crossed with theirs.

Charlie nodded unconvincingly. With every step it was becoming less distinct and more overgrown, and they were forced to ride in single file as she forged ahead on Pirate to clear a path.

They stepped carefully for a while, listening to the rain plopping heavily on the last of the brown and red autumn leaves that clung to the branches and bushes all around them, and the constant crackle and snap of twigs and branches beneath the ponies' hooves.

"Charlie, this *can't* be a bridleway," Mia said, peering down the gloomy, narrow way ahead.

"I thought you said there'd be a good stretch to canter," Alice commented as another bramble snagged her jacket so hard that she almost got pulled out of the saddle backwards as Scout kept walking forwards. Thunder rumbled again, only this time louder.

"No one in their right mind would want to

ride down here," Rosie complained, ducking down onto Dancer's neck to avoid branches. "Do you even have a clue where we are?"

"Erm, I think so," Charlie replied, knowing that, actually, she was totally lost and had no idea where this path was taking them. She rubbed her frozen hands together as Pirate ignored the spiky branches on either side of him. "I think if we just keep going a bit further..."

Suddenly, the bushes started to peter out and the shelter of the trees overhead thinned, exposing them to the lashing rain and allowing them to see into the distance. Ahead of them the path dipped down into a dense patch of wood.

"Look!" Mia gasped. "What's that?"

The others wiped their faces to get a better look through the heavy downpour.

"Ooh, I bet I know what it is," Rosie said, her voice going all quivery.

"What?" Alice asked, feeling goose-bumpy all of a sudden as she stared ahead.

"I... I think it's the Old Forge!" Rosie whispered loudly.

Lightning flashed in the sky ahead and thunder echoed above them. In the distance, beyond the dip into the woods, they saw a small, overgrown circular clearing. In the middle of the clearing, a stone barn rose up eerily out of the darkness. Its crumbling grey brick walls almost merged with the heavy sky as the rain swept down. One side was overrun with fading ivy and the windows were gaping black holes. Part of the moss-covered tiled roof was missing and one corner of the ancient, isolated barn had collapsed.

"Okay, so this is definitely not the way I meant to come," Charlie finally admitted. She shivered, and for the first time that day it had nothing to do with the cold.

"It's meant to be haunted," Rosie announced in a dramatic whisper that creeped them all out.

"Ghosts aren't real, Rosie – and that's a fact," Mia said, trying to convince herself as much as the others as the thunder rumbled again. "They're just made up in fairytales."

Wish, who was normally totally bomb-proof and responsive to the lightest of aids from Mia, suddenly snatched at the bit fractiously. She started to paw the ground, shaking her head as Mia touched the reins and gave her a pat.

"They are actually... Real, I mean," Rosie replied, pushing her soaked straggly hair out of her pink face. "I read about the Legend of the Old Forge in a book at school, for that project about local folklore we did last year, remember? Apparently, a blacksmith used to live all alone in the Old Forge in the days when a cobbled road brought him passing trade like coach horses to shoe. Then about a hundred years ago him and his huge black horse died, right here! The Forge fell into ruin and the rest of the forest closed in around it."

"It's not much of a legend," Alice said, feeling a bit disappointed in spite of being spooked at the thought of it being haunted.

"But that's not all," Rosie continued in a hushed voice, looking round at the others with her pale blue eyes wide. They all leaned in a fraction closer as Rosie dropped her voice to a whisper. "I read that when the wind's in the right direction, you can still hear the sound of metal being hammered, as the blacksmith makes ghostly horseshoes for his ghostly black horse!"

At that moment, darkness rolled in above them. Lightning lit up the skies and a clap of thunder broke overhead. The rain hissed down even more heavily.

Suddenly, a strange, eerie, spine-chilling neigh whispered through the air around them.

"What was that?" Alice squealed, her heart leaping as she and Rosie looked desperately at each other, their eyes almost popping out.

"It was just the trees creaking," Mia said unconvincingly. "Wasn't it?"

The noise echoed out again and Wish, already jittery, spooked and shot forward. Her back hoof slipped on the muddy path and she almost sat down before springing awkwardly back up. Mia was taken by surprise, and before she could stop herself she tumbled off sideways into a bush. Wish shoved past Pirate, clashing stirrup irons with him and squashing Charlie's leg. Charlie reached forward to grab Wish by the reins but just missed, and the frightened pony took off along the path ahead with a whinny, her ears pricked. Rosie stood up in her stirrups as Dancer snorted, watching the palomino mare disappear along the path ahead of them.

"She's heading straight for the Forge!" she cried, as Mia hauled herself out of the bush, completely covered in mud. Pirate and Scout danced on the spot.

"Come on!" Mia urged, red-faced after glancing down at how dirty she was. "I don't care if it's haunted, we *have* to go after her!"

The others gulped, but they knew that Mia was right. They squeezed their agitated ponies forward as Mia ran ahead, pushing back the bushes and brambles in her way, trying to keep her pony in sight.

Suddenly, Wish and the Old Forge disappeared from view as the path dipped back down into some woodland. Mia started to panic, worried about how scared her pony would be. She sprinted faster, tripping on tree roots, her long, silky black hair plastered to her neck and shoulders.

As Mia ran and the ponies jogged up the other side of the dip, the bushes fell away and they rushed into a clearing. The girls pulled the ponies up dead. Beneath their hooves were cobbles, slippery and almost hidden by the tall grass and mud – the only remains of the ancient road that used to run past the Forge. And just beyond the cobbles, as if in some kind of grim fairytale, out of the overgrown, wild grass rose the Old Forge itself. At the entrance nearest to them were two huge black doors. Mia felt her stomach tighten into a knot. There was no sign of Wish.

"Wish!" she called out. Her voice echoed in the creepy, heavy silence of the clearing. "Wish!"

"I don't think she'd have hung about here," Charlie said, staring towards the gloomy path which led away from the Forge on the other side of the clearing. "If she was frightened she'll have galloped straight past. I'll go and check."

Charlie jumped off Pirate and led him over to a little path that led away from the Forge. It was hard to make out any hoof prints among the tall grass near the ruin, but she definitely couldn't see a single one on the woodland path beyond.

"Anything?" Alice asked, swinging down from Scout.

Charlie shook her head. "Nothing."

Spooked, they all looked around, then Rosie pointed from Dancer's back.

"Hoof prints, look, there, they lead right up to…" Rosie gulped, "the Old Forge doors."

They all looked nervously at the ruin as Mia crept closer on wobbly legs.

"But the doors are closed!" Mia whispered hoarsely. "How could Wish have got in?"

Her heart had started to thump. She felt the blood drain away from her smooth olive skin as she looked round desperately, her dark almond eyes wide with fear.

"I can't see her, or hear her out here," Alice whispered, creeping nearer the ruin. "She *must* have gone inside."

"Maybe Wish went in there looking for shelter," Charlie said with a gulp as she followed Alice, "then the wind swung the door shut afterwards."

"You wouldn't get much shelter in there," Rosie said in a hushed voice as she hung back with Dancer.

"We'd better look inside though," Mia said, "just in case."

She edged towards the huge, wooden doors that led into the ruin. One was almost shut, but was hanging off its hinges at a slight angle, creaking in the wind. The other looked as if it hadn't been opened for years, with a slimy pile of sodden brown and yellowing leaves blown against it. Charlie and Alice crept up behind Mia. Rosie didn't dare creep any closer. She scanned the clearing, calling out to Wish in a hushed voice.

Suddenly, as the wind rose, a metal clunking sounded from within the ruin, a hollow noise which sent shivers through all of them.

"The blacksmith making his shoes!" Rosie squealed, gathering up her reins, ready to make a quick escape. "Quick, we have to go, like now!"

Mia's step faltered as she reached the slight gap between the two big doors.

"We can't go without Wish," she said urgently, feeling her heart race. As she peered into the gloom, terrified of what she might discover, the metallic ringing suddenly stopped. Mia gulped.

"Wish!" she whispered, as loudly as she dared, into the lifeless space.

She paused for a second, her legs shaking; behind her the clearing fell deathly silent except for the constant pattering of rain. Squinting through the heavy gloom, she saw a row of wide stables with ancient wooden doors, some closed and others creaking open as the wind whistled through. The far corner stables were cloaked in deep, cobwebby shadows. Mia stared harder into the darkness.

"Wish?" she whispered again, uncertainly. Suddenly she heard a dull thud coming from the shadows. A cloud of white mist briefly appeared above the end stall, before vanishing into the darkness. Mia gasped and whipped her head back out of the doors.

"There's.... there's the..." she stuttered, her voice failing.

"The what?!" Rosie demanded.

"The... the ghost horse!" Mia squealed.

At that moment a sinister, ghostly whinny cried out, soulless and hollow as it echoed around the Old Forge, filling the air. The girls looked at each other, petrified. None of them had ever heard anything like it before – it sounded like a noise from beyond the grave. At the same second a cold breeze swept past them. All the hairs on Mia's neck stood on end and her heart froze. There was a sudden stillness in the clearing, followed by a deafening crack as thunder split the sky right over their heads.

Mia heard a scream as she slipped on the slimy wet leaves in fright. She suddenly realised, as the ponies skittered in all directions, that the scream had come from her. As the thunder rumbled again she heard another whinny, this time much closer and much more real. Wish skidded round from the other side of the Old Forge, snorting and shaking her head. Mia grabbed her reins as the mare was about to barge past her. The ghoulish neigh rang out once more. Without another second's hesitation Mia leaped into Wish's saddle.

The others were already remounted, and within seconds they were trotting at full pelt back in the direction they'd just come from, pushing branches out of their faces with raised arms as Mia urged Charlie to go faster. Alice, still shaking, looked over her shoulder and saw Rosie, at the back of the pack frantically urging Dancer on faster as the roan's ears flattened and her eyes goggled, looking more frightened than the rest of them put together.

When they reached the end of the path, in sight of the lane, they were all so relieved to have got out of there that one by one they started to giggle and in a second they were all weak with laughter.

"Sorry, Mia… Who was it that said ghosts only exist in fairytales?" Rosie managed to say, after she caught her breath.

"Okay, so maybe I got that a bit wrong," Mia admitted, smiling, "but now I know that ghosts do exist, I never, ever want to go anywhere near there again! And nor does Wish – I've never seen her so scared!"

The rain started to ease slightly. Rosie claimed

everyone else had been far more scared than her, which set them off laughing again as they turned towards the warm and dry of Blackberry Farm.

Chapter
Three

TEN minutes later, the Pony Detectives were back on a familiar path, and after cantering around the edges of various fields linked by dirt tracks, gates and small jumpable hedges, they emerged onto a lane they'd ridden down quite a few times. As the ponies clopped along, heads down, they passed an isolated cottage. The girls saw a familiar face at the window and pulled up their ponies by the cottage gate. A second later, the front door opened and a girl with long dark-brown hair popped out and walked carefully down the path, carrying a kitten.

"Hi Daisy!" Alice grinned.

They all knew Daisy – she used to have a pony called Shadow, who was dark and devious and deposited her from the saddle at every opportunity when out riding. Shadow had been sold at the end of the summer to someone much more experienced, after one fall too many for Daisy. Since then, they'd bumped into her quite a few times, in town or when she'd been walking her dog in the woods where they were riding.

"What a gorgeous kitten," Rosie cooed as the others pulled up too just outside her front garden. "Is it yours?"

Daisy shook her head. "No, I've just started helping out at Hope Farm – the animal rescue place. Rolo here's the tiniest of the litter, and although she's been weaned she still needs lots of care, so Fran Hope has entrusted her to me."

The girls all exchanged impressed looks. They often went to shows at Hope Farm and knew how fussy Fran Hope was about who was allowed to help with her rescue animals.

"I go on Saturday and Sunday mornings," Daisy continued. "I decided that I want to be a vet when I leave school so it's really helpful. There are vets up there all the time because of the problems some of the rescue ponies have."

"That's amazing!" Alice smiled.

The others all crowded round to see the mewing bundle of tortoiseshell fur. Daisy nodded proudly, and it was obvious that she was loads happier than she had been at the start of the summer.

"I want to specialise in horses," Daisy said, a bit shyly.

"Please tell me you were not inspired by that menace, Shadow?" Rosie said, flabbergasted.

Alice, Mia and Charlie all glared at her.

"What?" she shrugged "I'm just asking."

"Definitely not!" Daisy laughed. "Although he wasn't to blame for me falling off him every five minutes, to be fair. But I do miss having a pony. Only trouble is that now I wouldn't have the time to look after one on my own, not with all the work at the vet's. Anyway, I'd better get Rolo back inside before she gets cold!"

With that Daisy said goodbye and the four girls set off again, trotting along various bridleways in single file until they got to one wide enough for the ponies to canter alongside each other. At least they could have done if everyone had kept up. Alice loosened her reins and Scout put his head down and leaped forward. Next to him Pirate fired along with Charlie balancing easily above him, her contact soft as Pirate poked out his nose, determined to reach the end first. Wish stretched elegantly beside them, easily keeping up as the part arab in her came out.

"Well, thanks very much for that!" Rosie puffed as she pulled up near the end of the path and slowed to a trot. Alice looked behind her as she patted Scout and started to laugh. Rosie and Dancer were completely splattered with mud; even Dancer's white blaze had disappeared beneath a layer of it. But, unlike Rosie, Dancer wasn't frowning. Instead, she shook her head and looked slightly confused, her ears flopping sideways as she skidded to a leg-splaying stop.

At that moment the heavens opened and the rain started to fall in great swirling sheets.

"Oh, perfect – that's all I need," Rosie sighed dramatically as they headed for home at a slow trot.

"I don't know what you're grumbling about," Alice smiled. "At least the rain'll wash the mud off."

Rosie couldn't help smiling at Alice as they turned the corner and reached the rutted drive that led up to Blackberry Farm.

"Look!" Charlie said suddenly, squinting through the rain at the old rustic gate that led to the little yard. "Someone's at the gate – I wonder what they want?"

Chapter Four

AS they got nearer they saw a girl hunkered down by the gate beside a propped-up bike. She looked about their age, wearing pale-blue jods and a padded pink jacket with a colourful stripy jumper poking out underneath. Her plaited brown hair was soaked, as if she'd been waiting for ages, and she was shivering in the cold, hugging a heavy-looking yellow canvas bag. She turned when she heard the ponies' hooves scrunching on the drive and looked slightly startled, almost as if she was going to make a run for it.

"Hi there!" Rosie called out cheerfully.

"Oh, you've only just got back from your ride," she said in a high, small voice, "I'll come back later. You must have loads to do."

She turned and walked back to her bike, with her head down, but Mia called out to her.

"That's okay. It won't take us long to put the ponies away if you can hang on five minutes. How long have you been waiting here, anyway?"

"Oh, only about... well... forty minutes maybe," the girl replied shyly.

"What? In this rain?" Rosie exclaimed, noticing how un-waterproofed her jacket looked. The girl nodded. "What's worth getting *that* soaked for?"

"I... I've got a bit of a problem," the girl said, pulling her coat closer around her. "I wondered if you might be able to help."

"What kind of problem?" Charlie asked.

The girl stood for a second. She opened her mouth as if she was about to speak, then she stopped and shivered, looking miserable.

"Why don't we put the ponies away first," Alice suggested. She was starting to really shiver too and wanted to get herself out of the rain and Scout rugged up. "It won't take long. Then we can go round to the barn and you can tell us what the problem is."

The girl nodded and dodged sideways while the others led their ponies past. She hung about, not quite knowing where to put herself as the ponies were settled in. Mia spent ages carefully inspecting Wish's legs, running her hands down them and checking for any cuts or signs of heat after her escapade. But her mare's legs were clean, much to her relief.

They dried their ponies off and put on their warm rugs over their sweat rugs, then left them munching happily on full haynets. Then they found the girl, who was standing out of the rain, just inside the feed room, and headed for the hay barn. The girl gazed at the pictures, rosettes and posters that had been pulled out of *Pony Mad* and stuck haphazardly over the barn's wooden wall while Charlie and Rosie hauled shut the big door to keep it as snug as possible. They climbed the ladder to the loft which was filled with sweet-smelling hay. If they squinted through the little gaps in the wood, they could see the yard below and the ponies as they bobbed their heads out under the eaves of the stable roofs every now and again.

With hay bales piled up around them to help them stay warm, blankets wrapped over their shoulders and an old sleeping bag covering their legs, the girls were really cosy. Mrs Honeycott, Rosie's mum, appeared, draped in a huge yellow mac with a big hood covering her paint-streaked hair. She was balancing a tray of steaming hot chocolates, along with a huge, still-warm banana cake for them to share – although they quickly discovered with a giggle that she'd forgotten to put any banana in. Mrs Honeycott had only made four cups of hot chocolate, so Alice gave hers to the new girl, and shared with Charlie instead.

"Are you sure you don't mind?" the girl asked, uncertainly.

"Course not." Alice smiled.

The girl thanked Alice, looking a bit awkward, then sipped from her cup nervously.

Once they were all settled with their drinks, she told them that her name was Pixie.

"Are... are you the ones who found Moonlight?" she asked hesitantly. She had dark circles around her eyes and her face was pale. The girls all nodded, glancing at one another. They had an inkling of what was going to come next. Even though they felt bad for Pixie, they couldn't help feeling the slightest rush of excitement about the possibility that she was bringing them a new case.

"My mum knows Moonlight's owners, not well or anything, but she said that I should come and see you with my... my problem," she continued. "Mum made me promise I'd come here, but I didn't want to bother you, not if you're really hectic with big cases – you're probably way too busy to help, aren't you?"

Pixie glanced up, looking almost as if she was waiting for them to agree, so that she could disappear.

"Well, it's true, we do always have big cases on

the go – that's the nature of being a successful Pony Detective," Rosie lied.

"But we can always make room for one more," Mia added quickly, glaring at Rosie, who hid behind a huge bite of cake.

Pixie sighed quietly and her shoulders drooped as she gazed at the floor. "Mum said you'd probably say that."

"So what's the problem?" Charlie prompted her.

"It's my horse – Faraway Phantom," Pixie said dully. "He's disappeared."

"Dish-appeared?" Rosie asked through a mouthful of cake. "Really?"

Pixie glanced up at Rosie, then looked away. "Well, he's gone missing at least."

Mia pulled out her notebook from behind one of the bales, then started to write, her head down, and her long black hair falling neatly over her shoulders. Even after being drenched, Mia still somehow managed to look immaculate. When she'd got up to speed, she waited with pen poised for Pixie to go on. But she didn't.

"When did it happen?" Charlie prompted, as Pixie fiddled with the strap on her bag.

"Um, yesterday – Saturday," Pixie replied quietly. "One minute he was there, and the next he was gone... no trace."

"There's always a trace," Rosie said knowingly, tapping the side of her nose and not realising that she had cream from her hot chocolate on her finger.

Pixie looked slightly scared for a second. "Is there?"

Rosie nodded. "Even when people think a case is unsolvable, the Pony Detectives pick up on the tiniest clues. And what do they find?"

Pixie gulped. "Er, ponies?"

"Well, technically, yes," Rosie said. "That, and *success*. Success is our middle name."

"Er, that's good news." Pixie half-smiled, before looking down at the hay-covered floor again.

"So, going back to Faraway Phantom..." Mia said, chewing her pen.

"Oh, that's his show name," Pixie explained in a small voice. "I just call him Phantom."

"Okay, so can you tell us exactly what happened yesterday? I mean, like when you noticed he'd gone, stuff like that?"

Pixie thought for a second. "I got to the yard in the morning at my usual time, which was pretty early, and he… well, his stable door was open and he'd just gone. He can open the top bolt and if he kicks the door he can flip open the bottom bolt too. Bit of an escape artist, you see. Normally I always put the lead rope clip on the bolt so he can't but… well I'm *sure* I did but I can't be a hundred per cent certain. Maybe I forgot…"

"What does Phantom look like?" Alice asked.

"He's 15 hands high," Pixie said, "and black."

"Any markings?" Mia asked, head down, writing.

"Um, he's got a star and half a white blaze over his nose."

"Anything else?"

Pixie shook her head then sat quietly for a second.

"Do you know his breeding?" Rosie asked.

"Oh, yes – he's three-quarters thoroughbred and a quarter Welsh," Pixie said, putting down her mug and looking over towards the loft ladder.

"Was he wearing a rug?" Charlie asked.

Pixie nodded. "A purple one, with light purple piping."

They all agreed that at least he wasn't wandering around the countryside in the cold and wet totally exposed to the elements. Being part thoroughbred he wouldn't have a nice thick coat to help him keep warm.

"Age?" Alice asked, after waiting to see if Pixie was going to speak in the silence that followed. She frowned, finding it increasingly odd that Pixie was being so quiet. They were having to extract information from her piece by piece. Alice knew that if she had been describing Scout, it would take her at least two hours to go through all his best bits, not two seconds, and she wouldn't need any prompting.

"Six. And a half," Pixie replied before glancing at her watch and standing up. "Look, I'd better go, it's getting late. And, honestly, I know Mum's all worried and she wanted me to come and everything, but if you're really busy with other stuff then, well, it doesn't matter. I'll just tell her that. It's okay."

The others looked at each other, frowning.

"It doesn't sound okay," Mia replied. "In fact, a thoroughbred cross running round in this weather sounds like an emergency to me. We'll get onto it right away."

"Oh, right, of course," Pixie said. "Thanks."

She slung her bag over her shoulder and walked towards the ladder.

"Have you got a photo or anything we could look at?" Charlie asked, thinking that they would need it because they had very little else to go on.

"Not on me," Pixie said, looking worried.

"I could bring you one though."

Mia suggested that she could drop one off the next day after school.

"Erm, okay," Pixie said hesitantly, then started to climb over the top of the ladder.

"Oh, one more thing," Mia called out just as Pixie was about to disappear. "I almost forgot – where was Phantom stabled?"

A cloud crossed Pixie's face.

"Compton Manor," she replied, looking down as the girls all exchanged glances.

"Funny, we were there earlier," Mia smiled.

"I guess you think I'm lucky to have Phantom stabled there," Pixie said quietly, gripping tightly on the ladder. "Everyone else seems to think so."

"I might have done up until we visited," Mia replied. "Now I'm not so sure."

Pixie looked up, and for the first time seemed to relax for half a second.

"Oh, and what's the CM club?" Alice asked before Pixie disappeared. "I heard someone there talking about it."

"You mean Sasha, right?" Pixie asked. Alice nodded. "It's the Compton Manor club. It's very exclusive, and you've got to earn your way to being Sasha's best friend to be in it, which basically means you have to do everything she says when she orders you around, including all her mucking out and grooming. Oh, and laugh at her horrible jokes."

"And at other people when she's mean to them," Alice finished.

Pixie nodded.

"If you're not in her club, she makes life pretty miserable. Trouble is, she runs the place, for the Under 16s anyway," Pixie sighed despondently, "and her mum's always so busy she hasn't got time to listen to any of us if we go and complain. Sasha gets away with *any*thing, there's nothing anyone can do about her. Anyway, I guess I don't have to worry about that any more. Look, I really have to go now."

The girls called out goodbye, then waited until they heard Pixie's light footfalls pattering out of the barn.

"Sounds like she had a horrible time at Compton Manor," Mia said, re-reading the notes she'd made.

"That's hardly surprising, with Sasha running things," Rosie agreed.

"But, apart from that, does anyone else think that Pixie was acting weirdly?" Charlie asked. "I mean, I know she came to see us, but I reckon that was only because her mum *told* her to."

"Exactly, not because she wanted to," Alice agreed.

Suddenly they heard a skidding of hooves outside on the concrete and all the ponies started to neigh at the top of their lungs, as if one of them had got out of their stable. Beanie appeared from nowhere, barking territorially.

The girls looked up and stared at each other for a second. Then, without saying a word, they flew downstairs and out of the barn, slipping on the loose hay that covered the floor as they raced round the corner to the stables. There, outside the gate but clambering back over it to safety, was a petrified Pixie. In front of her, head raised high, stood a wild-looking pony.

Chapter Five

IT was the pony's appearance that made him look wild, rather than anything he was doing. That and the fact that Pixie was staring at him as if he was some kind of demon from the dark side. He was covered in a thick layer of caked-on mud, his mane and tail matted with it, and his cobby face was pinched. His eyes had a look of desperation in their dark depths, asking for help almost as clearly as if he'd spoken to the girls. His fluffy ears were out sideways and he was wearing a muddied blue headcollar with clogged-up holes, which looked like it had been there for a while.

As the pony looked over at the girls he didn't panic and run away, but stepped closer to Pixie, uncertainly. Pixie shrank away from him, looking paler than before. The pony reached his nose out to her, but Pixie squealed and moved quickly out of the way.

Rosie looked from the pony to Pixie. "I don't believe it! Is that Phantom?" she asked, disappointed that their case might be solved before they'd even had a chance to look for a single clue.

"No!" Pixie squealed. "I've never seen this pony before!"

"Are you sure?" Alice asked, as she stepped past Pixie and took hold of the pony's headcollar. "It's hard to tell what he looks like under all this mud."

"I'm sure," Pixie insisted.

"How weird's that, then," Charlie said, confused. "Phantom goes missing one day, and a pony turns up out of nowhere the next."

"I don't recognise him. Do any of you?" Alice said.

The others shook their heads.

"What are we going to do with him?" Mia

asked as Alice blew into his large nostrils gently before running her hand down his neck. The pony turned and rubbed his head on her, almost knocking her over.

"We'll have to see if we can find out who he belongs to," Charlie said.

"I know – why don't we ask Daisy," Rosie suggested. "If she's helping out at Fran Hope's rescue centre she might have information about missing ponies, that kind of thing."

"Good idea," Alice agreed. "I'll call her." As Alice pulled out her phone the runaway pony frisked her pocket for treats, his little eyebrows raised. Suddenly a large rumbling echoed in him.

"But first," Rosie added, "we'd better get him something to eat."

"And we can't just leave him out here and hope he finds his way back home," Mia said, unable to stop herself from smiling, "so we'll have to get the spare stable sorted!"

"What, you're just going to put him in one of

your stables?" Pixie asked incredulously. "I mean, won't you get into trouble for doing that? Don't you have to ask someone?"

"This isn't Compton Manor," Rosie joked. "I doubt Mum will even notice – she's normally in a world of her own, but she'd approve anyway. She'd never want to see an animal without a home in this weather."

Pixie's face suddenly fell.

"Don't worry, though," Mia said, as Rosie went pink, realising what she'd said. "It won't get in the way of us trying to find Phantom, too."

Pixie wiped her light brown hair off her face, nodding.

"Although it's obvious you're going to be pretty busy now, so, you know, don't worry too much. Anyway, I'd better get going," she said, dodging past the pony hastily. She grabbed her bike from where it had been leaning against a nearby bush, jumped on and began to pedal down the lane.

"Don't forget the photo tomorrow!" Charlie called out while Alice led the pony into the yard.

"If she comes back at all," Rosie said under her breath, wondering whether they'd seen the last of Pixie, who didn't really seem to want to be there in the first place.

Mia found a spare lead rope and clipped it to the runaway pony's headcollar.

"I wonder where he's come from?" Alice asked.

"Well, wherever it is, he wasn't looked after very well there," Mia concluded disapprovingly as she patted his neck.

"Hmm, maybe, but look." Charlie bent down and picked up one of his front hooves, wiping it with her hand. "His feet aren't overgrown and his shoes don't look that old, so he can't have been left alone for too long, thankfully."

He stood and looked round at the other ponies as they pressed against the front doors of their stables, curious about the newcomer. Then he watched the girls' every move, his eyebrows still up, as they rushed round sorting out his bedding, hay and water. Alice called Daisy and explained what had happened.

"We get notices and pictures about missing ponies sent in all the time," Daisy told Alice, sounding excited. "I'll come over now. I might recognise him!"

Alice put her phone away, then suddenly noticed some blood coming through the mud on the pony's near hind leg. He looked round to watch while Mia quickly checked it.

"I don't think it's too bad," she announced, standing up. "We just need to wash his leg so we can get a better look."

She tied the pony up in the yard outside the spare stable, and while Rosie hosed his leg, Mia offered him a drink. He dipped his muzzle into the water, sloshed it around, then drank deeply before Mia took the bucket away. She didn't want him to have too much all at once in case it gave him colic. Once the bucket was gone, he instantly turned his attention to the bulging haynet that Charlie and Alice had hung for him. The pony tore great mouthfuls from it, gulping it hungrily as if he hadn't eaten properly for ages. Finally, his little eyebrows relaxed and his eyes softened, the desperation starting to leave them.

The girls set about grooming him, tackling the dry mud and leaving the wet stuff, trying to comb through the mud matting his mane and tail. The pony stood quietly resting his back leg. He looked around with his dark eyes as he munched his hay, huge trails of it hanging from his lips as his teeth ground rhythmically. By the time Daisy arrived a blue roan pony with white patches had emerged from under the mud. He had feathers, and cobby legs and hooves, and a large, honest head with a white face.

Daisy rushed into the yard, beaming.

"Isn't he adorable!" she breathed. He turned to look at her, leaving his hay for a second so that he could frisk her pocket for treats. When he realised she hadn't got any, he turned his attention back to the haynet. Then she saw his back leg, which Rosie had hosed clean. She bent down next to it to inspect the wound. The pony flinched slightly.

"It's only a surface scrape luckily – nothing serious," Daisy announced. "It needs an antiseptic rinse, then some purple spray, I'd say."

The others exchanged surprised glances. Daisy looked and sounded so confident. Mia ran to the tack room to fetch the first-aid kit and handed it to Daisy. Daisy sorted through the kit, then rinsed the cut out with some antiseptic. She dried the leg gently and put some purple antiseptic spray on it.

Charlie untied the patient and led him into his freshly laid stable. Daisy took off his headcollar and checked underneath. There were a couple of raw spots where it had rubbed, so she put some wound powder on them.

"What about a feed?" Rosie asked, bringing

over some more hay to refill his net. "He obviously needs one."

"Just hay for the moment," Daisy recommended as the pony pulled at Rosie's armful while she tried to shove it in his haynet.

Daisy stood for a moment, patting the pony. She bit her lip. "I don't recognise him from the posters up at Hope Farm," she finally said, "but I'll ring Fran when I get back, in case an owner turns up between now and when I go there next Saturday. I'll let you know what she says. Anyway, I'd better get home to see to Rolo. Is it okay if I pop back, though, to check on the pony?"

"Of course!" Alice smiled. "And thanks for your help, Daisy."

Daisy smiled. "No probs!" Then she hurried across the yard, grabbing her bike on the way out.

Mia turned to a new page in her notebook and wrote down 'Runaway Pony' with a big question mark. She jotted down his colour (patchy blue roan), his height (about 14.2 hands high) and that he was a gelding. Charlie aged him roughly and Mia wrote that down too (around sixteen years).

"We don't really have a clue about him," she sighed. "We've no idea if anyone's looking for him, or if his gate was left open by mistake – nothing."

"He could even have been stolen, then dumped," Rosie suggested.

"Or maybe he escaped his field because there wasn't much grass," Charlie suggested, "or water. That might be why he's so hungry, and it could explain the cut on his leg."

"Good point," Mia said, a making note of all the possibilities.

"But if Daisy doesn't find any information at Hope Farm," Rosie said, "where will we start?"

"Right now," Mia said, "I don't really know."

"Poor pony," Alice sighed. "He could have been wandering about in all that rain for days."

"We'll have to think of a name for him,"

Charlie said. "We can't just call him 'poor pony' all the time."

"How about Puzzle?" Rosie cried out. "Because right now he is one!"

"Perfect!" Mia said, wishing she'd come up with it.

"Now we just have to solve the puzzle," Charlie said. Suddenly the Pony Detectives had two new cases – the runaway pony and Phantom. Charlie patted Puzzle and smiled. From now on they'd be so busy that she wouldn't have a second spare to worry about Pirate's future.

Chapter Six

CHARLIE and Alice normally cycled together to Blackberry Farm before school, while Mia got dropped off by her dad. But on Monday morning Mia persuaded her dad to take a detour so that he could give them all a lift. They'd wanted to get there extra early so they could check on their new arrival after his first night. Rosie had texted them all evening with updates, but they couldn't wait to see him for themselves.

Before they got into their usual, hurried, pre-school routine of feeding, watering and refilling haynets along with skipping out the worst of the droppings, they'd rushed to Puzzle's stable. He stood looking over his stable door brightly and contentedly, loving all the fuss that followed.

After promising him they'd return as quickly as possible, and Mr Honeycott saying he'd keep a close eye on him while they were at school, they'd sprinted off, with hay on their coats and covered in horse hair, to catch the school bus.

They spent their lunch hour poring over a map of local bridleways.

"This is the first time we've ever had two cases to handle at the same time, and we need to decide which one's our priority," Mia said as she bit into her apple. "I think it ought to be Phantom. I know we need to try and find Puzzle's owner, but at least he's safe and warm at the moment. Phantom, on the other hand, may not be. He's got a rug, I know, but he's thin-blooded and he may not have food or water. So we have to try and find him first. Does everyone agree?"

The others nodded.

"Mum and Dad are going to call the local police too," Rosie added, "to see if they've had any reports of stolen ponies who match Puzzle's description."

"Good," Mia continued, drawing a big purple circle on the map. "So now we can concentrate on Phantom. What we need to do is look in the areas near Compton Manor. We should make a list of the stables around there and then divide the area so we visit a few each evening. He's likely to have headed towards a yard, I'm guessing."

"Like Puzzle," Rosie agreed.

"Exactly, so that's where we should start our search over the next few evenings, before it gets too dark after school," Mia continued. "And for Puzzle, I think we should ride round this weekend to see if we can find any signs of a pony escaping from a field, or owners who are out looking for a lost pony."

"And what happens if we do find a likely field?" Charlie asked, happy that the next few days were looking seriously busy. "There might be loads of possible matches. And the owner's not going to be just hanging about there, are they?"

"Aha! I thought of that," Mia said, starting to

write out a note in her best handwriting. "I'll get Dad to photocopy this, then we can put up signs."

"I can ask Mum to put one up in the local post office, too," Rosie offered. "Hopefully someone will see it and recognise him."

FOUND!
Blue roan cob pony with white patches,
approx 14.2hh, around 16 years.
Being stabled at Blackberry Farm.
Please contact the Pony Detectives
for more information.

They all agreed to put Blackberry Farm's phone number at the end of the note, then Mia slid it into a clear plastic folder, ready to photocopy and take with them on the rides when they went hunting for clues to Puzzle's background.

Later that afternoon the Pony Detectives rushed out of the school gates as soon as the home bell rang. After the school bus dropped them off they raced straight to the stables, bursting to see how their new pony was settling in since they'd left him that morning.

Puzzle bobbed his head out, ears pricked, as the girls ran into the yard. He stood happily as they fussed around him. He already looked ten times less sorry for himself than he did the day before – he wasn't cold or miserable and frightened any more, but seemed relaxed and happy, and he fitted in so well that it felt as if he'd been there forever.

As they patted him they heard another set of footsteps hurrying across the yard. They thought at first that it might be Pixie, but it was Daisy, making a beeline for Puzzle's stable.

"I've come to check on the patient," she beamed, armed with a bagful of chopped-up carrots and apples.

The others pulled on their riding clothes and their hi-vis jackets and jodhpur boots.

"We're going to start our search for Pixie's horse, Phantom, over by Compton Manor," Charlie told her. "Are you okay to stay here with Puzzle so he doesn't get upset when the ponies leave?"

"Definitely," Daisy replied, looking enthusiastic about having a pony to look after again. "I'll give him a groom and sort out his stable while you're gone. Oh, and I called Hope Farm last night to see if anyone's reported a pony like Puzzle missing, but nothing so far."

While they were starting to get the other ponies ready and tacked up, Pixie wandered shyly into the yard. She went to a different school from the Pony Detectives and was still in her uniform, but she had a huge, floppy jumper on over it. Her hair was loose apart from two plaits at the front which were pulled back and tied behind her head. She smiled nervously as Alice told her they were heading out to start their search for Phantom.

"I've brought a picture," she said, keeping her distance as Alice led Scout out of his stable.

Alice looked at the grainy, slightly out-of-focus photo. It had been taken at Compton Manor and showed a stunning black horse, with Pixie holding on to the end of his lead rope. The horse was turning away from the camera but he towered above Pixie and she looked anxious. Although the picture wasn't great, it was clear that the horse was top quality.

"He's gorgeous!" Alice said admiringly, tightening Scout's girth and pulling down the stirrup irons with a leathery slap.

Pixie nodded. "I guess."

"Must have been expensive!" Mia commented as she led Wish over to them and Alice handed her the picture. Pixie blushed slightly and said quietly that he was. Rosie whistled as the photo was passed to her. Mia took the photo back and studied it hard.

"Funny, he looks a bit like a horse at the yard I bought Wish from – Clover Hill Stables," she said. "Did you get him from there?"

Pixie looked surprised. "Oh, I... I'm not sure. He was a present, so..."

She edged away from the ponies, looking scared as Pirate pulled at his bit, unable to stand still. She twiddled her hair.

"How's the runaway pony by the way?"

"Puzzle?" Charlie replied. "Oh, he's doing really well."

"You can go and see him if you'd like," Alice said, wondering what Pixie was so frightened of, considering that she had her own horse. "He's in that end stable with the vet."

Pixie opened her eyes wide.

"Not a real one," Rosie added.

"Not yet, anyway," Daisy said, leaning over the stable, smiling. "I could do with a hand checking this cut if you've got a mo."

Pixie looked unsure.

"I can't stay long," she said.

"It won't take long," Daisy replied decisively, not taking no for an answer. Pixie reluctantly agreed, dropping her bag outside the stable and opening the door slowly.

The other four walked their ponies out of the yard into the dampness, their hooves scrunching on the stony mud. They headed for the first area Mia had marked on the map, covering a big distance as they rode round to three yards which were all some way from each other.

But after trotting round for ages all they discovered was that no one had seen a black thoroughbred with a purple rug wandering loose. Mia gave each yard her number, just in case they did find him, and everyone they met promised to keep a lookout.

"Still, it's only the start of our search," Mia said, trying not to feel disheartened.

They couldn't stay out too long because the dusky evening was turning darker by the minute. After hurrying back to Blackberry Farm they found Daisy still chattering away to Puzzle, who'd been thoroughly groomed. She said that Pixie had gone not long after they'd set out on the ride.

"I wonder why she rushed off?" Alice asked.

"Or why she didn't want to wait and see if we had any news of Phantom." Charlie added.

"Maybe she'll turn into a pumpkin if she stays out too late?" Rosie suggested. Pumpkin, the ginger yard cat, came running out of the tack room, hearing his name mentioned. She picked him up and hugged him. "I wasn't talking about you, silly."

It was the same pattern over the next few evenings, with the four Pony Detectives riding round in the dusky half-light searching for Phantom while Daisy looked after Puzzle. Although they hadn't suggested it, and she didn't bring any new information about Phantom with her, Pixie turned up every night, too. She crept in quietly, interested in how Puzzle was getting on. She never once asked how the search was going, but she stayed a little longer each time, helping Daisy and gradually doing more and more of the grooming and feeding. Then she'd disappear into the damp dusk on her bike before the others got back.

By Friday the four girls were feeling decidedly less optimistic about finding the black horse when they hacked out after school. The weather was still fairly grim, but they kept going, spurred on by knowing how thin-coated Phantom was, rug or no rug. They only had a few stables to check in the final area of their search.

The first two yards weren't far from Compton Manor, set on the edge of the trees not far off the lane. But for the last one, they had to head into the heart of the woods. Mia had purposely left it till the end, hoping that they'd have found Phantom before they reached it because it took them into the area near to the Old Forge. After the way Wish had reacted last time, Mia didn't want to go anywhere near it.

The yard was tiny, with only a handful of stables filled with older, retired racehorses. To get to it they had to ride through the woodland along the narrow paths that criss-crossed the one Charlie had led them down by mistake. They found a small dirt track that cut through the trees and followed it. The branches overhead creaked in the wind, making Alice tense. Scout started to spook at things hidden in the gloom that Alice couldn't even see. That set off Pirate, who scooted into Wish. Mia, already on the lookout for scary goings-on, squeaked while Rosie and Dancer just goggled at everything and anything.

By the time the Pony Detectives stepped up to the yard gate, thinking that they'd never want to stable their ponies in such a remote spot, they were all frazzled. But there were no sightings to report from there either.

"The horses have been a bit more unsettled in the last week, though," the yard owner said, "almost like they're hearing things that I can't – you know what horses are like, standing there with their ears pricked, looking into the dark. I'm sure they do it to scare me most of the time."

The owner laughed, but her suggestion of an unseen presence near the Old Forge didn't make the girls feel any less spooked. As they walked their ponies back onto the dirt track, Alice saw Scout's ears suddenly flicker and he grew taller, snorting and backing into the others.

"Careful," Rosie squeaked as Dancer was shoved and almost tripped.

A light appeared out of nowhere, bobbing along one of the narrow paths which cut across the one they were on.

"Someone's up there," Alice whispered urgently to the others, her hands shaking. They all stopped dead.

"Or some*thing*!" Rosie breathed. "Coming from the direction of the Old Forge! Quick... we need to go!"

She tried to turn Dancer, who stubbornly refused to budge, her eyes out on stalks watching the light.

"Hang on," Charlie said, squinting into the

semi darkness through the overhanging branches, "I think it's just a bike headlamp."

The next second, Charlie was proved right as the bike hurtled towards them and Alice called out in surprise. "Pixie!"

Pixie looked up from under her huge, flapping hood and almost fell off her bike as she skidded to a rapid halt.

"You made me jump!" she cried.

"What are *you* doing here?" Rosie asked incredulously as Dancer took the opportunity to grab a mouthful of leaves from a nearby low-hanging branch.

Pixie opened her mouth for a second, then closed it.

"Well, it's kind of obvious, Rosie," Charlie said, looking at Rosie as if she was mad.

Pixie looked between them. "Er, it is..?"

"Looking for Phantom, same as us, right?" Charlie said.

"Right," Pixie said, glancing down. "I wanted

to keep searching myself, too."

"Well, we've checked all the yards around Compton Manor," Mia told her, pulling out her map and list to show Pixie. Pixie looked as if she was holding her breath.

"But so far, nothing," Alice sighed. Pixie breathed out.

"Have you got any other ideas where Phantom might have headed?" Mia asked.

"Not really," Pixie said, frowning. "I mean, he could have galloped miles away by now. We're probably wasting our time looking here. There's nothing around."

"Just the ghost-filled, spookified and haunted ruin of the Old Forge," Rosie whispered. Charlie thwacked her with a stick, trying to smile but still feeling the shivers go up her neck.

"Oh, I didn't go anywhere near there," Pixie said, shaking her gloveless blue hands and blowing on them. "I just went down a little bit, but there were owls and things rustling through the bushes and stuff, so I came straight back. It was way too scary. I didn't reckon it was worth going any further anyway. I know there's nothing else down there, from hacks I went on from Compton Manor. Everyone used to avoid this part of the woods. I don't think even Phantom would be silly enough to head down here. How about you – have you got anywhere else to check tonight?"

"No, we're heading back now too," Rosie replied as Dancer swung her bottom round, this time planting herself most definitely in the direction of home.

Pixie smiled for a second. "If you follow this path," she said, pointing to a narrow one to their right, "it should bring you out of the woods."

She waved goodbye and they watched as her light bobbed off towards the road. Once she'd disappeared they walked their ponies along the dirt track.

"How does that make sense?" Rosie asked, shaking her head.

"What?" Charlie and Alice asked in unison.

"Well, this might sound odd considering she's got her own, but Pixie seems terrified of ponies," Rosie said, confused. "Yet she'll happily cycle around in the dark near the Old Forge, by herself! You'd never catch *me* doing that!"

"I guess that shows how much she wants to find Phantom," Alice said, although she did think Rosie had a point. "And she does know all the bridleways and paths around Compton Manor too, remember."

"Doesn't explain why she's so scared of ponies, though," Rosie mumbled as Mia led them down the path leading off the dirt track which Pixie had pointed out. It quickly took them to the edge of the woods and out alongside some fields. Scout took a step to one side to avoid a root and Alice scraped her leg against a fence, her jodhpurs catching on something sharp.

"Ow!" she cried out, making Scout shoot forward, his ears back. She pulled him up and looked across the dusky gloom into the field.

"Hang on, guys!" Alice called. "Look at this – it's a broken fence. Do you reckon this could be Puzzle's field?"

As Alice rubbed her leg the others gathered round. Mia pulled her powerful torch from her pocket and swept it slowly across the field. It was muddy and waterlogged, with a few patches of ancient-looking grass. There was a water trough, but the ground around looked marshy, as if the trough must have a leak. And they noticed that there were no other ponies in the field and no signs of hay being put out to make up for the shortage of grass. Leading to the piece of broken fencing were long, rain-filled hoof skid marks, which had dug deep into the ground and scuffed up what little grass there was.

"It looks like a pony's tried to jump out here," Charlie suggested, "then skidded on the slippery ground and crashed into the fence, cracking the wood. That might fit with Puzzle's injury."

"Possibly," Mia said, uncertainly. "I guess it *could* be his field."

"If it is, it would explain why he wanted to escape," Rosie sighed.

"We might as well put a note up here, just in case," Mia said. She got out one she'd been carrying round in a plastic, rainproof cover and tied it to the gate, taking the baler twine through the hole she'd made in the cover so that it was securely fixed. "All we can do now is keep Puzzle snug and well fed and hope that this might be the right field. If it is, then his owner will see our note and ring."

"Although if any owner kept a pony in a field like this," Rosie grumbled, "I don't know if I'd want him to go back to them."

"Either way, we've got signs up for Puzzle now – here and at the post office," Charlie said, "but what do we do next about Phantom, considering this search has got us nowhere?"

"I reckon we need to go back to the beginning," Mia suggested. "Back to Compton Manor where he disappeared from in the first place. Someone there must have seen *something*."

"It's getting too dark to go now," Rosie pointed out, "but at least it's the weekend tomorrow, so we'll have time to ride over."

Alice and Mia agreed. Charlie sat quietly as the ponies trotted towards Blackberry Farm, thinking that Compton Manor was the last place she wanted to go if Sasha was going to be around. But then, if it helped solve the mystery of Phantom's disappearing act, she'd just have to ignore Sasha and get on with the business of being a Pony Detective.

When the girls got back they said hi to Daisy and Puzzle and put the ponies away. Each girl quickly flicked over their pony's coat, picked out their hooves into skips and rugged them up snugly, checking their haynets and water before going to the feed room to make their dinner.

"That's odd," Alice said as she opened Scout's feed bin. She dipped the feed scoop in but the level had gone down more than she was expecting.

"Have you taken any pony nuts for Dancer?" she asked Rosie. Both of their ponies ate the same type of nuts and sometimes they used each other's if one of them was getting low. But Rosie shook her head, opening her own bin and frowning.

"Even odder," she said. "Mine have gone down too."

"Puzzle's been having a small handful each evening," Daisy said.

"I know," Alice replied, "but it's still gone down more than I was expecting, even taking that into account."

That evening, after they'd fed and said good night to the ponies, they all began to wonder whether they had a third mystery on their hands: the case of the missing pony nuts.

Chapter Seven

"GET those jumps down, Bex," Sasha shouted over her shoulder as she trotted The Colonel out of one of the big indoor schools. "Er – hello! Like, today! Honestly, you're so slow sometimes."

"Sorry Sasha. I thought you said earlier that you wanted me to leave them up?" Bex said, sounding confused as she hurried towards the school.

"Whatever. Now I'm saying that I want them down," Sasha huffed, making a face at Bex as if she were stupid, "so hurry up."

While Bex rushed inside to see to the jumps, Jade stood smirking at her, patting The Colonel.

"I don't know why you're laughing. You should be in there helping her," Sasha sniffed as she dismounted.

"Oh, right, 'course," Jade said, looking caught out.

"Only joking," Sasha cackled, throwing her reins at Jade. "Here, take Colly and untack him for me. Make sure you brush him over, too."

Jade forced a smile and led the sweating chestnut away. He was so exhausted that his back hooves scraped along the concrete, as if he was too tired and his muscles ached too much to be able to lift them properly. And he wasn't even being given a warm down by the looks of it.

Charlie leaned forward on Pirate and peeped around the door to the school. A whole course of massive fences had been set up inside. Sasha slid the door shut with a slam, spooking the ponies.

"Oh, you're back again," she said, turning her gaze on the four girls in front of her, narrowing her eyes as she looked at Charlie. "I see your pony hasn't grown, but it looks like you have. Anyway, what is it this time? Have you messed up your entry forms or something?"

Mia gave a fake smile, wanting to say that her handwriting was perfectly neat, thank you very much, but she kept her cool.

"No, we've come to ask you about a horse called Phantom," she said. "He used to be stabled here, until last Saturday."

"Ha!" Sasha burst out, laughing meanly. "That useless black maniac? Good riddance to him. What do you want to know about him? I could tell you lots. Follow me."

Sasha headed off towards the empty office. Rosie, Mia and Alice followed her while Charlie happily volunteered to stay outside and hold the ponies. Sasha shoved some money into a vending machine in the corner and a can of fizzy drink crashed to the bottom. She picked it up, cracked it open and flung herself down on one of the sofas, swinging her leg casually. The other three stayed standing up, and Alice leaned back against a wall of photographs. As they were talking she glanced at the pictures and noticed one of a fine black horse with a star and a distinctive white half-blaze.

"It's just that Pixie…" Mia began. At the mention of her name, Sasha snorted. Mia cleared her throat and started again. "It's just that Pixie said he went missing from here last weekend. No one's seen him since."

"Really?" Sasha said, sounding bored. "I thought he would have turned up somewhere by now."

"Where?" Alice asked.

"I don't know, anywhere," Sasha said, frowning. "Mind you, he's a stupid, freaky horse so he's probably wandering about in circles somewhere, scaring everyone witless. Either that or he's finally got fed up with his useless owner and decided to get as far away as possible from her."

"Pixie's not useless!" Rosie retorted before she could stop herself, going pink. "She happens to be very nice!"

Sasha looked over at Rosie, sizing her up, before she took a big glug of drink. Then she leaned forward as if she meant business.

"Listen, I don't know what she's told you, but I'm glad that lunatic horse isn't here any more," she sneered. "This is meant to be a competition yard and he couldn't win if he was the only horse in the class. He used to spook at everything – he'd rear all the time. He was a nightmare, full stop. And Pixie couldn't do anything with him – she was terrified. That's not the kind of rider we want on this yard, simple."

"And I bet you told her that, didn't you?" Mia said, shaking her head.

"I tell the truth. If people don't like it, they know where to go," Sasha scoffed. "That nutcase horse was taking up a stable that a better horse could have had – we've got a waiting list of top-quality riders as long as my arm. And I don't actually see what all the fuss is about. It doesn't make much difference him going last weekend because he would have been chucked off the yard any day now anyway."

The girls looked at each other, confused. Sasha smiled.

"Pixie didn't tell you *that* bit, did she?" she said smugly. "Okay, well *I* will then. Her dad paid for Phantom's first six months of stabling when he dropped him off here. That ran out a week before Phantom went missing. He's been given a reminder but no one's heard a peep from him about paying any more, not even Pixie."

"How do you know?" Alice asked.

"I overheard Mum leaving him a voicemail about owing money, so I checked her file to find out for myself. I saw that payment was overdue. I had a word with Pixie, that was all. She snivelled a bit, told me about not hearing from her dad for a while, but it's not *my* problem, is it?" Sasha said, leaning back in the sofa. "I just told her to find a cheaper stable somewhere else. I *may* have given her a helping hand by getting Jade to take the clip off Phantom's top bolt last Friday night when no one was around. He can let himself out of the stable without it. How was I supposed to know the stupid beast would wander right out of the yard and get himself completely lost?"

"He probably couldn't wait to get away from here!" Rosie cried. "And, for your information, there's only one stupid beast on this yard, and it hasn't got four legs, it's got two!"

With that Rosie stormed off to the door, swung it open and marched through. Straight into the cupboard with all the brooms in. As Sasha burst out laughing, Rosie turned on her heel and marched back out, bumping straight into Alice and setting Sasha off into a fresh wave of snorting and giggling. Rosie huffed, then stomped to the other door. The right door, held open for her by Mia. The other Pony Detectives closely followed their friend back onto the yard, without a backward glance at Sasha.

"Can you believe her?" Rosie ranted, as she climbed back into Dancer's saddle and they trotted the ponies down the drive, away from Compton Manor.

"So because of a prank, a valuable, hot-blooded

horse is wandering about the countryside in the worst weather!" Charlie said, amazed that even someone as mean as Sasha could act so thoughtlessly.

"Although I still think it's a bit strange," Mia mused. "It might be one thing to let a horse out of its stable, but why would that horse leave the yard it's been stabled in for six months and just disappear out of the gate?"

"Maybe he's still on the grounds here somewhere," Charlie suggested, looking round. It was certainly a big enough place.

"No, Sasha's reaction when she heard he hadn't turned up anywhere was honest enough," Alice said. "I think she would have smiled horribly or something if she'd seen him around here somewhere."

"It still doesn't add up, though," Mia frowned. "Pixie may not like this yard but there'd be no reason for Phantom to stray, even if he was let loose. He's fed here."

"And even if he did stray," Charlie added, "where's he strayed to? We've checked all the yards around. It's like he's vanished into thin air."

Alice fished something out of her pocket. "I nearly forgot," she said, wiping the dust off the picture with her arm and passing it to Charlie. "While Sasha was distracted by Rosie's antics with the doors, I managed to get this from the wall."

"See?" Rosie cried triumphantly, still fired up. "Once again my intuition has helped us further a case!"

"Right, Rosie, you walked into the broom cupboard on purpose," Charlie laughed, passing the photo to Mia. "We believe you."

"Hang on a second," Mia said, staring at the photo of a striking, fine black horse with a star and a distinctive white blaze which started halfway down his face. "I thought I recognised this horse when Pixie brought that first picture in but I couldn't see his face properly, so I couldn't be sure. Now I know it's *definitely* the horse that was kept at the same competition yard as Wish. They were the top two ponies of the yard at the time and were totally best friends. They were stabled next to each other and always grazed alongside each other in the paddock."

"But Sasha said this one's useless," Charlie said, looking confused as she tapped the photo. "Are you sure it's the same pony?"

"Definitely," Mia said, thinking hard. "I mean, I only saw him briefly when I went to try Wish, but it's definitely him – he was the kind of horse that leaves an impression. I didn't ride him because I wanted a show pony and he was one hundred per cent a jumper. He had huge scope over fences. I saw him being ridden, and he looked really difficult. I could imagine him being a handful unless you were totally confident and experienced."

"Which Pixie isn't," Alice added. "And that's kind of what Sasha was saying, although she put it in a much meaner way."

"Pixie doesn't strike me as the competitive type." Rosie frowned. "So I don't get why she bought Phantom in the first place."

"We may find the answer to that question at Clover Hill," Mia suggested, pulling out the map from her pocket. "It's a bit of a trek, but I reckon it'll be worth it, just in case."

Chapter Eight

"I RECOGNISE that pony!" Mrs Millar, the owner of Clover Hill Stables, boomed as she walked bow-legged towards the gate with a huge smile, her grey hair pulled back into a hairnet beneath her velvet riding hat. "Wish Me Luck! How's she doing? She looks a picture! What a lovely surprise!"

Mrs Millar gave Wish a hearty slap on the rump, startling the mare, who dipped her back end, her ears out sideways. Then, Mrs Millar turned to Mia and gave her a crushing hug before asking them to come on in, sizing up and appraising the ponies as she spoke.

The girls dismounted and led their ponies into

the small, weathered but tidy yard. A couple of the helpers recognised Wish and ran over to say hello, wanting to hear all about her. Mia was happy to update them, listing the highlights of her winning sequence since buying the palomino a year and a half ago.

After the helpers had patted and fussed over Wish, saying how nice it was to see her and Mia, they jogged back to their hectic round of preparing the horses on the yard for exercise. When the helpers had ridden out on two of them, Mrs Millar asked the girls to walk with her as she got her next horse, a flighty three-year-old, ready to lunge.

"Mrs Millar… Do you remember a horse you had on the yard called Faraway Phantom?" Mia asked, pulling the photo out of her pocket. She stood back as the horse in the stable squealed, his ears pricked while Mrs Millar calmly and coolly busied around him.

Mrs Millar's eyes lit up. "Of course I do! Young horse, quirky to sit on, had a difficult background before I got him, but a real superstar over a fence."

Mia nodded and the other girls grinned at each other, realising they'd made the right decision to come to this yard.

"Went to Compton Manor quite recently," Mrs Millar said, pausing for a second and looking at the girls. "He's not for sale again already, is he? I had him here for another year after you bought Wish, you know. He wouldn't have suited everyone. I only sold him, what, must be six months ago now."

"No, he's not for sale," Mia explained, "but he's escaped from Compton Manor, and we, well, we were hoping he might have somehow made his way back here, considering he knew the place."

Mrs Millar shook her head, a look of concern on her face.

"Good thought," she agreed, "but sadly not. Well, I'll certainly keep my eye out for the poor chap, and give you a ring if I see him. I hope he's going to be okay if he's wandering about in this weather. He's a light-conditioned horse, easily unsettled and always worrying his weight off at the best of times."

The girls looked at each other: that was exactly what they'd feared.

"What did you think about Pixie, the girl who bought him?" Charlie asked. "How did she get on when she tried Phantom?"

Mrs Millar shook her head. "Didn't see the girl – Pixie, did you say her name was? Yes, I remember that now. No, her father came, nice enough chap but not really horsey. Said he wanted a top competition horse for his daughter, said that money was no object, he wanted the best. Said the horse would be going to Compton Manor, where his daughter would be able to have lots of lessons from experienced competition riders, and they'd promised to help her with whichever horse he bought." Mrs Millar paused to tuck a strap into its keeper on the horse's bridle.

"I wouldn't normally have sold a horse without seeing the rider", she continued, "but I'd called Compton Manor myself and spoken to Mrs Compton. She'd assured me that her daughter, who was in charge of the Under 16s yard, would personally look after Pixie and would report any problems straight to her. I offered to come over and give Pixie lessons myself, but Mrs Compton said that they'd take care of everything. I was convinced, and Pixie's father said his daughter was a very good little rider, anyway."

The girls exchanged glances, thinking that he'd clearly exaggerated a bit.

Mrs Millar opened the stable door and the girls stood back as the youngster bounced out of his stable on his toes, skittering sideways. The girls followed at a distance.

"Anyway, got to get on. Was there anything else at all?" Mrs Millar asked, paying attention to the huge, playful chestnut on the end of the lunge line as she led him to the school.

"No, that's it. Thanks very much, Mrs Millar," Mia called out.

"Well, let me know when you find him, won't you?" Mrs Millar said genuinely, before pausing a second and looking over at Charlie. "And let me know if you'd like me to fix you up with your next horse. I've got some lovely ones at the moment. About time you moved up to something bigger, I'd say."

Charlie's mouth dropped open for a second, and she put her arm defensively around Pirate's neck and hugged him to her. Pirate leaned back against her.

"Phantom," Mrs Millar said, as she strode out to the school, "very distinctive, what with his—"

At that second her mobile phone rang and she fished it out of her pocket. "Got to go, girls. Lovely to meet you all. Stay in touch! Hello? Mrs Millar speaking…"

The girls remounted. Charlie put Pirate in the lead and he jigged forward, eager to be off.

The others looked across at each other, then at Charlie.

"Listen, Charlie, about what Mrs Millar said..." Mia began.

"She was really helpful about Phantom, wasn't she?" Charlie said, smiling too brightly.

"Er, yes..." Mia said, "but that wasn't what I was talking about. I meant—"

"I know what you meant, but I don't get why everyone suddenly wants to talk about me and my pony, especially when we've got much more important things to worry about," Charlie said, more sharply than she meant to. "We need to focus on the reason we *actually* came here: Phantom."

Charlie's eyes glistened just for a second before she cleared her throat. "Pixie's dad has been mentioned a couple of times now," she continued, making it crystal clear that Mrs Millar's comment about her getting a new horse was not up for discussion.

Mia shrugged to Alice and Rosie. They

guessed that if Charlie wanted to talk about it, she would, so they changed the subject.

"Right. So what do we know about Pixie's dad?" Alice said, as Charlie rode slightly ahead, staying quiet.

"We know now that he bought Phantom without Pixie being there to help choose him," Mia said, "which fits with Pixie not knowing he came from Clover Hill."

"And it sounds like he set her up at Compton Manor," Alice added.

"But then he seems to have disappeared soon after," Rosie said. "Maybe her parents split up?"

"Possibly," Mia agreed. "That might explain a few things. Anyway, Pixie knew that her time was up at Compton Manor, thanks to Sasha, so where was she going to take Phantom next? She must have had a plan. I mean, it sounds like she could've been asked to leave any day."

The girls rode in silence for a moment.

"I wonder why she didn't tell us about any of

that stuff?" Alice asked. "I mean, it's kind of relevant, isn't it?"

"Maybe she felt embarrassed?" Rosie suggested as they continued speculating on the way back to the yard. "Anyway, it doesn't really matter, does it? Phantom's still missing, either way."

But all their discussions kept coming back to Pixie and the lack of detail that she'd told them about the case.

"The trouble is, Pixie keeping stuff back might be getting in the way of us finding Phantom – we just don't know," Mia said as they reached Blackberry Farm and slid out of their saddles, just as the rain started to fall again. "I think we need to go back over the details we have so far."

They quickly put the ponies away, rugging them up and checking that they had full haynets and water buckets. Then they rushed round to the hay barn, sliding the door shut and climbing up into the loft as the rain started to patter more heavily on the roof above them. Alice shivered and pulled a rug over her shoulders, as Mia got out her notebook and flipped to the page with Phantom's name at the top, adding the details from Mrs Millar and Sasha.

"Look, Pixie has given us very little information so far," Mia pointed out, showing the others the page. "It's just basic stuff about what Phantom looks like."

"Everything else has come from what we found out today," Charlie said, looking a bit less glum now that everyone was concentrating on the mysteries again.

They looked down the list that Mia had written below Pixie's description of Phantom and his disappearance.

Sasha:
a) clearly made life miserable for Pixie at Compton Manor
b) said that Pixie was terrified of Phantom and she had difficulty riding him (the

photo shows her looking scared just
standing next to Phantom)

c) told Pixie that her dad hadn't paid up
   the next lot of stabling fees

d) made it clear she didn't want Phantom
   on the yard

e) took headcollar clip off his stable door,
   letting him escape (Why would he leave
   the yard? Where did he disappear to?
   No yards nearby have seen him...)

Mrs Millar:

a) said that Pixie's dad chose Phantom
   for Pixie without her even trying him

b) said that Pixie's dad said money was
   no object (but then he hasn't paid
   stabling fees???)

c) said Phantom was a quirky ride (ties in
   with what Sasha said)

"Pixie could have told us all of that right at the
start," Alice said, reading through it.

"It's almost as if she doesn't *want* us to find Phantom," Rosie suggested. "But why?"

"I'm not sure she's even missing him," Charlie added after a short silence. "Maybe, just maybe, if she was as scared as Sasha said she was, and Phantom's as much of a handful as Mrs Millar described, then she might even be relieved that Sasha set him loose."

"Especially if she didn't have a clue where to stable him after her time was up at Compton Manor," Alice agreed.

At that moment there was a squeal of bike brakes. As Puzzle whickered a welcome, they knew that Pixie had arrived.

Chapter Nine

AS the girls emerged out of the hay barn and into the yard Pixie skipped across without noticing them, beaming as she headed straight to Puzzle's stable. She was getting more and more confident with him, probably because he was very quiet and affectionate, unlike the description they'd got earlier of Phantom.

Although it was raining, Pixie was like a ray of sunshine in her yellow waterproof jacket and pale blue jods, with her yellow bag and a long, multi-coloured scarf wrapped around her customary plait. Minutes later Daisy arrived, after her dad dropped her off at the end of her morning shift at Hope Farm.

"I'd really love another pony," Daisy sighed as

she joined Pixie in Puzzle's stable and they began grooming him. "If I could have one like Puzzle, I'd be really happy."

"Me too," Pixie said dreamily, giving him a hug, before looking suddenly guilty and backtracking. "I mean, I love Phantom, it's not that, I… I just meant that if I *didn't* have Phantom, then Puzzle's the kind of pony I might like."

Charlie, who had been standing at the door, tickling Puzzle's drooping lower lip, glanced up. Pixie blushed, distracting herself by grabbing the spare bridle Mia had adjusted. Puzzle had put on weight since getting to the yard, and they'd decided that, as his leg was healing brilliantly, they'd see what he was like to ride. Then, if he was okay, the next morning while Daisy was at Hope Farm Pixie could join the other four and ride him on a hack. They were going to the field where they'd put up the notice, to check that it was still in position.

Pixie slipped the headpiece over Puzzle's ears

as he lowered his head for her, and gently slid in the bit. Then she led him out of the stable. They hadn't put a saddle on because they didn't think any of theirs would fit well enough not to rub or press him in the wrong places.

The other five girls had voted that Charlie, the bravest of the riders, should be the first to sit on Puzzle. Charlie had happily agreed, and Rosie had legged her up onto Puzzle's broad back. Charlie felt the warmth of his sturdy body as she wrapped her legs around him. He was a hand taller than Pirate at 14.2hh, but Puzzle felt much bigger because he was very chunky and cobby and her legs had to stretch much further to get round him.

Charlie squeezed Puzzle. That would've been enough to send Pirate into an immediate speedy jog, but Puzzle took a moment longer to respond. After a second or two's delay, he walked steadily out into the muddy ring in the schooling paddock behind the stables. Charlie walked him on both reins, making sure that he was warmed up before squeezing him into a trot. At first nothing happened, so Charlie asked again, this time more firmly, and he popped into a slow, comfortable trot. His ears flickered back and forward as he listened to Charlie. She smiled, thinking how short-striding and speedy Pirate's trot was compared to Puzzle's.

She asked him for a canter and he bobbed forward. Charlie sat easily on his broad back as he cantered steadily and slightly lazily, his pink nose poking out just a bit. Then after a circuit of the ring Charlie squeezed on the reins and he fell back into a trot. She re-balanced him and rode him over to the others, who were sitting on the fence huddled up in their jackets as they watched.

"He's so sweet!" Charlie beamed, patting Puzzle. His ears pricked, and he got mints offered from all sides. "He didn't put a hoof wrong. He's a bit stiff at the moment, but that's not surprising. I reckon he hasn't been ridden for a while, but he's been nicely schooled in the past – it wouldn't take long to get him going really well again. Daisy, Pixie, do either of you want to have a go on him?"

Pixie almost fell off the fence as she pushed Daisy in front of her, and Daisy almost fell off in her eagerness to have a go. Charlie legged Daisy up while Puzzle stood quietly, looking round as she landed gently on his back. She walked him round and even tried a little jog, but then started laughing and nearly slid off, so she brought him back to the fence.

"Come on, Pixie," she said, "even *I* felt safe up there, and that's saying something. He really is lovely to sit on."

Pixie didn't look convinced, but the others persuaded her and she suddenly gave in.

"Okay, okay!" She smiled, and hopped off the fence. "I'll do it!"

Charlie gave her a leg-up and stood beside her to begin with. Pixie looked anxious and jittery, tipping forward and holding her reins far too tight, so much so that Puzzle raised his head, a confused look on his big, honest face. Pixie squealed nervously, looking as if she was going to get off. But Charlie just told her to ease up on the reins and, when she did, Puzzle dropped his head and stepped forward. It wasn't long before Pixie started to radiate happiness as sunny as her yellow raincoat as she went round. Once she'd relaxed and realised that Puzzle wasn't going to do anything scary, it became clear that she was actually a good rider, just like her dad had told Mrs Millar.

Pixie rode over to them, beaming.

"So, all set for the ride to the field tomorrow, then?" Rosie asked, jumping off the fence and patting the contented cob. Everyone looked at Pixie expectantly, including Daisy, who was having to miss the ride.

"Er… I guess I am!" She laughed, leaning down along Puzzle's neck and putting her arms around him. He pricked his ears as everyone gave him lots of fuss, and Rosie was convinced that he was smiling as they led him back to the stables.

U U U U

On Sunday morning the heavens opened, and it wasn't until nearly lunchtime that it finally eased up and the five could set out under a sullen sky. They agreed to ride at a walk the whole way to the field as Pixie didn't have a saddle. After her trial ride the day before she looked totally relaxed from the start. As Puzzle strode happily along, his fluffy ears pricked and his eyes bright, it seemed like a million years ago that he'd turned up looking wild and abandoned. His coat was already so much better from all the grooming and fuss that Pixie and Daisy had given him.

They eventually turned onto the bridleway alongside the edge of the woods, which led to the field where they'd pinned the notice. The path started off with enough room to ride two abreast between the woods and the fencing, and Mia and Alice led at the front, followed by Rosie. Behind them Pixie rode along next to Charlie.

Pixie glanced sideways as Charlie took her feet out of the stirrups, letting her legs hang down.

"You're going to need longer stirrups soon," Pixie smiled.

"Or a bigger horse," Charlie replied with a huge sigh, "as everyone keeps telling me."

"Oh, sorry, I didn't realise..." Pixie said, looking awkward for a second.

"No, it's okay, I didn't mean you," Charlie said quietly. "But you're right. Everyone's noticing how tall I'm getting, and Pirate here isn't growing with me, are you, boy?"

Charlie leaned down and hugged Pirate's chunky bay neck. He flickered his ears back for a second, then pricked them forwards again.

"So what are you going to do?" Pixie asked.

"Well, I've tried not thinking about it," Charlie smiled brightly, acting as if it was no big deal. But as she looked up at Pixie's pale face and sympathetic eyes she realised that she wasn't fooling anyone, least of all herself. She sighed heavily. She knew she finally had to face what was happening. "The trouble is I can't afford to buy another horse without selling Pirate, but there's no way I'd ever do that. I'd rather not ride at all and keep him, but I don't know if that's fair on him. Everything seems really muddled at the moment. I feel totally stuck, and I don't know what to do next."

"I know how *that* feels," Pixie said quietly, twisting Puzzle's mane in her fingers as above and around them drizzle began to patter down heavily. Charlie glanced at her and was about to ask why, when Mia pulled up Wish just ahead and called out to them.

"The notice is still here."

The ponies gathered round the gatepost. The notice was flapping in the breeze in its plastic covering, but looking slightly weathered.

"And we haven't had any calls yet," Alice sighed. "So I guess no one's seen it yet, either."

They stood and looked at the notice for

a second, wondering what to do next. Then Wish suddenly raised her head and stared into the woods. She let out an ear-piercing neigh and broke into a trot, following the path as it disappeared into the trees. The mare ignored Mia as she sat into the saddle and squeezed the reins to bring her back to walk.

"Wish!" Mia said, using the reins a bit harder until her mare begrudgingly listened to her and waited restlessly for the others.

"Is she okay?" Pixie asked as they caught up. The rain was starting to fall more heavily while the skies darkened above, making the path even gloomier.

"Hang on a sec!" Rosie gulped, starting to panic. "If we follow this path deeper into the woods, it'll take us close to..."

"The Old Forge!" Alice said, feeling the hairs stand up on her arms as Wish let out another shrill neigh.

Mia looked at her mare – Wish's caramel-coloured ears, darkened and dripping with rain, were pricked, her head high.

"Maybe we *should* go back there," she said, unsure, as they stood gathered in a bunch on the path inside the woods. "I mean, Wish seems to think we should. We can have a really quick look and then head back, that's all."

"That's all?!" Rosie squeaked. "That won't be all when we're racing away from here again and one of us gets left behind and sucked up by the ghouls! It's all right for you – you're on a fast horse. Think about me and Pixie – she hasn't even got a saddle to cling onto if Puzzle gets spooked!"

"Rosie's right," Pixie suddenly piped up, looking whiter than a sheet as she sat rigidly on Puzzle at the back of the group. "I... I don't really fancy heading down there. It's a seriously scary place. I think we should stop right now and go back."

"Maybe Mia's got a point, though." Charlie shivered as Pirate stomped his front hoof impatiently. "I know it's spooky, but we could just take a really quick look...?"

At that second Wish let out another shrill neigh and shot forward, staring into the gloom of the path. The other ponies followed instinctively, then suddenly there was a loud cry behind them. They quickly pulled up and turned to see Pixie sitting on the muddy ground, holding her left wrist gingerly. Puzzle was gazing down at her with big questioning eyes. Charlie immediately jumped off Pirate and knelt down next to Pixie. After prodding Pixie's wrist gently, making her yelp, Charlie stood back and sighed.

"I'm not really sure," she said uncertainly, "but Pixie can still move it quite a bit, so it could just be sprained."

"What happened?" Alice asked, looking behind her.

"I... I don't know," Pixie said, shaking her head. "I think Puzzle must have been spooked by Wish. He just kind of jumped forward a bit when the other ponies set off and I slid sideways..."

The others looked quizzically at each other, then at Puzzle. He didn't seem like the kind of pony to be spooked by anything.

"He was most likely terrified by the ghost horse," Rosie agreed.

"We should probably get back," Mia said, looking at Pixie's white, scared face.

Charlie legged Pixie back up onto Puzzle, then jumped onto Pirate. Mia battled to turn Wish away from the path, with the mare raising her head and fighting for a second before she swung her quarters round with a sigh, her ears grumpily turned out sideways. They took it really slowly because of Pixie, but almost as soon as they reached the lane she seemed to get some colour back in her face and looked less pinched as she rode along with her left arm tucked into her jacket as a makeshift sling.

By the time they got back to Blackberry Farm the rain had just about stopped. Daisy was there waiting for them, and she helped the girls get their ponies settled in their stables, out of the moaning wind. They left the ponies cosily tucked up in their rugs, munching on their hay.

The ride home had taken longer than they'd planned because they could only walk and had to take it really slowly. As they all headed over to the feed room Pixie seemed unsettled as she checked her watch.

"I'd better go," she said, standing by the door for a second. "See you all tomorrow."

"Regular as clockwork," Daisy smiled. "She leaves at the same time every day, almost to the minute."

"Hang on!" Rosie suddenly called out as she noticed something by her feed bin. "Pixie! You've forgotten your bag!"

Alice picked up the canvas bag to pass it out to Pixie. It felt strangely heavy. And it *smelled* familiar. Alice was about to lift the flap and look inside when Pixie dashed back and grabbed it with her left hand.

"Thanks," she said, smiling awkwardly for a second before she headed back out and ran over to her bike. As Alice watched from the doorway, she saw Pixie glance anxiously over her shoulder.

"Did anyone else just notice that?" Alice whispered as she watched Pixie disappear up the drive.

"What?" Rosie asked, frowning.

"Pixie just picked up her bag with her left hand," Alice said, turning back to the feed room. "And her wrist seemed absolutely fine."

"Really?" Charlie asked. "That bag looked heavy too."

"It was," Alice said, taking a deep breath. "And I think I know why."

Chapter Ten

AT school on Monday, Rosie yawned as she pulled a bit of hay out of her tangled hair. She was sitting with Mia, Charlie and Alice in their form room after lunch, avoiding the rain outside, as they went back over Alice's theory from the evening before.

"Pony nuts? You're absolutely sure, Alice?" Mia asked for the third time.

"Like I keep saying, I didn't have a chance to look *in* Pixie's bag," Alice repeated, "but it *smelled* like pony nuts and it was really heavy. Like it was full of them."

"But what's she doing with them?" Rosie asked. "Eating them? They don't taste very nice – I've tried them."

"Why doesn't that surprise me?" Charlie joked.

"Maybe she took them to use as a treat when she went out on her own looking for Phantom. You know, for when she found him?" Alice suggested.

"A whole bagful?" Mia said, doubtfully. "And if your and Rosie's pony nuts have been going down as much as you say, that can't be the first lot she's snaffled away."

They sat quietly, looking at Mia's notebook now they'd added Alice's new clues.

"And you think Pixie might not have hurt her wrist, either?" Mia said, almost to herself.

"Well, if she did," Alice said sceptically, "it recovered very quickly afterwards – that's all I'm saying."

"So, basically, you reckon Pixie faked it," Charlie said grimly. "Although, to be fair, she really didn't want to go to the Old Forge. Maybe that was her only way of getting us to turn round?"

"When we were out looking for Phantom the other night, we bumped into Pixie looking too," Rosie said. "She'd been near the Old Forge then, but she'd turned back because she was scared, remember? Maybe she'd just been seriously spooked that night."

"So spooked that she faked her own injury to avoid going back there." Charlie nodded. "It's possible, I suppose."

"I hate to say it, but the Old Forge keeps cropping up," Alice said with a shiver.

"I know," Mia said grimly. "So maybe it's time we found out a bit more about it. And I can only think of one way to do that."

"Please tell me you're not about to say what I think you are," Rosie said, putting her head in her hands. "It's madness. The place is totally freaky."

"We *need* to find out what's behind all this," Mia said. "So, tonight after school before it gets too dark, I vote we revisit the Old Forge. Agreed?"

Rosie groaned as Alice and Charlie took a deep breath, then they all nodded.

U U U U

The girls jumped off the school bus and rushed to the stables straight after school. They quickly gave Puzzle some fuss, checked his water and refilled his haynet, then hauled on their hi-vis riding gear and got tacked up.

"Daisy and Pixie will be here pretty soon," Alice said. "We should let them know where we've gone, otherwise they'll wonder why the place is deserted when they arrive."

"Okay, I'll text them," Mia said, as they jumped into their saddles and rode out of the yard. She pulled out her phone and wrote a message:

Gone to Old Forge to investigate, sorry to leave Puzzle on yard alone, but sure you'll be there to keep him company soon!

They headed out into the drizzly, grey late afternoon, armed with torches and a flask of hot chocolate, which Rosie had phoned ahead to ask her mum to make. Mia had rolled her eyes, muttering that they wouldn't have a chance to drink it, but Rosie had slotted the flask into her rucksack beside some torches.

They rode along the path that they were beginning to know with their eyes shut, and the ponies seemed bored at being taken in the same direction once again.

"Hopefully, Dancer, this will really and truly be the last time," Rosie told her mare, who huffed as she sluggishly clopped along. "Possibly because we'll all die of fright. You have to promise that if anything happens to me you'll carry me home safely, like a loyal friend would. Got it?"

Dancer snorted and shook her head.

"Very loyal, thank you," Rosie sighed.

Charlie led the group, with Mia just behind. Alice and Rosie rode side by side for as long as they could while they rode past the field where they'd pinned Puzzle's notice. But as they turned onto the path into the woods, they had to go back to riding in single file.

The girls fell silent as the path they were on crossed with the overgrown one that led to the Old Forge. They turned onto the overgrown path, concentrating as they rode through the biting brambles, and pushing branches out of the way. Alice's heart was already starting to thump and her legs felt as jelly-like as they always did before she was about to go out and jump at a show.

Wish started to get agitated well before the Old Forge came into view. And when the ruined building did finally emerge from the gloom, seeing it for the second time didn't make it look any friendlier. A bat flew out of the dusk, fluttering past them and making Mia jump out of her skin. Then the ruin disappeared momentarily from view and they rode back into the thick clog of wood.

As Wish danced back out of the dip, bunny-hopping into the clearing, the sun dropped below the skyline. For a moment the sky turned a dusky, bruised blood red. Mia patted her mare, whose ears were pricked forward, as she dismounted.

Wish pulled at her reins, her delicate hooves skidding on the almost hidden ancient cobbled lane that cut across in front of the Forge. She whickered powerfully, deep within her throat. The sound was echoed back – hauntingly, hollowly, ringing around the clearing – just as Rosie, Alice and Charlie slid out of their saddles and landed on shaking legs. At that moment another bat brushed past Mia's head. She squealed, closing her eyes and ducking. Then she screamed as she felt a tug on her arm.

"Quick! This way!"

Mia opened her eyes to see Charlie by her side. Rosie and Alice were ahead, trotting their ponies into the edge of the woods on the other side of the clearing and hunkering down.

Hurriedly, with shaking hands, Mia dragged a mulish Wish behind Charlie and across to the others. They all huddled together, the trees sheltering them from the rain as they looked out into the fading light.

"Er, so what do we do now?" Rosie squeaked as Dancer tried to reach some foliage behind her and planted a huge saucer-like hoof on the end of her riding boot.

Suddenly a mobile phone chimed loudly into life, making everyone, including the four ponies, jump. Mia fished out her phone and read the text message.

"It's from Daisy," she whispered, then read it out:

> **At yard now, Puzzle fine. Pixie**
> **txted 2 say she couldn't make it**
> **2 yard 2nite, didn't say why.**

"Maybe she realised I knew she'd taken some

nuts yesterday," Alice said, feeling bad suddenly, "so she couldn't face coming in just in case we said anything."

"Maybe, but we'll have to deal with that later," Mia said, taking a deep breath. "Right now, we're here, and if we're going to do this properly I think a couple of us need to go inside the Forge, while a couple of us stay out here with the ponies. Any volunteers?"

"You never mentioned anything about us having to go inside!" Rosie hissed, her eyes almost popping out. "There is no way I'm putting even a TOE inside that place, and I don't fancy hanging around while anyone else does either – what if they go in and don't make it back out? In fact, rather than sitting here wondering what's going on I vote we make our escape, like, yesterday!"

Wish raised her head, staring into the clearing. Charlie looked over at her. Suddenly she frowned.

"Hang on though," Charlie said to Rosie, gazing at the mare.

"For what, exactly? Because, just so we're clear, there's no way I'm hanging about if there's the slightest risk that me and Dancer may become ghost fodder!" Rosie whispered urgently, trying to keep her voice down so it wouldn't attract the attention of any nearby ghouls. She got hold of her stirrup, ready to remount.

Suddenly the clearing was filled with the spine-chilling echo of a sad ghostly neigh. At once they were deafened by Wish's neighing reply as her nostrils fluttered wildly and her body shook with the force of it, right next to them. As Mia struggled to hold her, Rosie squealed and immediately ducked back down with the others, her heart rocketing as she grabbed hold of Alice.

"See!" Rosie whimpered. "Wish has got the right idea, she wants to get away too! She knows a ghost when she hears one!"

But while Mia gripped Wish's reins, stopping her from charging back into the clearing, Charlie stared at the palomino mare. Her ears were pricked hard. Then it clicked. Charlie passed Pirate's reins to Alice.

"Do you know what?" she said. "I don't think Wish is desperate to get *away* from the Forge. In fact, I think she's desperate to get *into* it!"

"Why would she want to do that?" Mia asked, confused.

But Charlie didn't wait to answer. She scooted forward through the rain towards the ruin, her feet slipping on the cobbles as she crossed the old lane.

"Charlie! Come back!" Rosie called frantically behind her. "Don't sacrifice yourself!"

Ignoring Rosie, Charlie crept up to the huge black doors that loomed out of the darkness in front of her. One door still had a huge windswept pile of orange and red autumnal leaves heaped against it. In front of the other one, the one that was slightly ajar and hanging off its hinges, there was a fresh scrape of mud, as if it had been hauled open. Recently. Charlie's heart started to thud hard in her chest. She looked across the gloomy clearing to the anxious faces of the others. Rosie waved frantically at her to come back. But instead Charlie started to pull on the door that was already ajar.

It scraped open with a low groan and she slipped inside, ignoring Rosie's pleas for her not to be so daring (or it might have been 'stupid', she couldn't quite hear). She stood for a second by the entrance, letting her eyes get accustomed to the dark. Inside, the ruin smelled dusty and dank, like wet stone and rat droppings. Charlie heard scuttling noises around her. Without warning, a dark shadow swooped silently down from the roof beams, gliding just over the top of her head, making her hair stand on end as she froze to the spot, her breath halting for a second. She whipped round to see a huge brown barn owl disappear silently through the doors. She breathed out, slowly, looking down. Then she saw something on the floor. It looked familiar.

Charlie picked it up and examined it. She frowned.

"I didn't realise ghost ponies ate pony nuts," she said out loud, trying to make herself feel braver as she pocketed her find and stepped quietly through the ruin. As she moved between the old, falling-down stables on one side and tools and ancient straw on the other, the ghostly whinny greeted her again. She stopped in her tracks. Now she was closer it sounded more anxious and scared than ghoulish and sinister. Charlie squinted through the damp half-light, feeling her way towards the dark shape in the end stable. A stable that was bolted shut, with a lead rope clip on the front.

Charlie approached quietly, talking softly under her breath. At that moment she heard the familiar plop of droppings landing on straw, followed by the distinctive smell. A rather un-ghostlike smell, she thought to herself as she got closer. There, standing before her was the most beautiful horse she'd ever seen – a black horse wearing a purple rug, his head held so high that he looked enormous. He arched his powerful neck down towards Charlie, nervously blowing hard on her hand.

"Charlie!"

Charlie jumped as she heard Rosie's voice and turned towards the door.

"Are you still in there? Have you been eaten by the ghost? Answer me! What's going on in there?!"

"It's all right," Charlie called out, her voice echoing round the hollow building as the black horse shied backwards, the whites of his eyes showing as he raised his head. A head that had a striking white half-blaze. "I've found Phantom."

Chapter Eleven

"SO all the time I thought Wish was terrified by the Forge, she was actually trying to get to her old best friend!" Mia said after they'd hauled open both doors and led their suspicious ponies out of the rain and into the ruin.

Wish had dragged Mia straight down the centre of the Forge until she'd stopped outside Phantom's stable and the old friends had reacquainted themselves, nickering through their fluttering nostrils.

"Wish's behaviour makes sense now," Alice agreed, "but Pixie's doesn't. I don't get it – she asked us to try and find Phantom but she knew where he was all along."

"And she put us off finding him, twice,"

Charlie said, thinking about the time they'd bumped into her on her bike near the Old Forge and when she'd come for the ride at the weekend. "Falling off Puzzle was a sure-fire way to make us turn back so we didn't reach the Forge. That way she managed to keep her secret, with Phantom hidden away from where anyone could find him."

Charlie stood by Phantom's delicate head and tried to calm him. They looked round at the dismal home the nervous black horse had lived in for the last week. His smart leather headcollar with its engraved brass nameplate looked totally out of keeping.

"The question is," Rosie said, "why?"

At that second the door creaked.

"I can answer that," a faraway voice whispered. The girls whipped round and saw a silhouette framed in the doorway. It was Pixie.

ᴗ ᴗ ᴗ ᴗ

Rosie poured a cup of hot chocolate out of her flask, looking pointedly at Mia, and saying that she'd known it would come in handy. She passed the cup to Pixie, who took a gulp of the hot, sweet drink. Pixie looked up at the girls' expectant faces.

"I know you must all think I'm mad bringing a horse like Phantom here – any horse here – but I didn't know what else to do," she explained, as Phantom continued to be fractious. Charlie slipped into his stable to stand near him. "I was so miserable and scared that I couldn't even think straight. It... it all started when my mum and dad split up nearly a year ago," Pixie gulped, then carried on. "Up until then Dad had taken me riding every weekend – it was something we always did together. I used to joke about wanting a pony and he'd always smile and say, 'One day, Pixie, one day' – although I knew deep down we could never afford it. Then, after they broke up he got a job in New York. I guess he felt really guilty, because just before he left he took me to

Compton Manor and there, in a stable with a pink bow on the door, was Phantom. Dad said he was all mine."

Pixie sighed.

"But nothing could make up for Dad moving to America, and things seemed to go wrong from the moment he left. Mrs Compton told me Sasha was going to look out for me, and to go to her with any questions. Only, Sasha made me feel really unwelcome from the second I arrived. At first she kept saying that Phantom was too good for me, and that I was a rubbish rider. I didn't really know how to look after a pony and Sasha wouldn't help – all she did was laugh at me. Then she started to say that I'd turned Phantom into a horrible, useless horse. It felt like I was doing everything wrong and I ended up dreading going each day. It wasn't what I expected it to be like at all. It wasn't small and friendly, like the riding school where I learned to ride, or Blackberry Farm."

"So why didn't you just change stables?"

Charlie asked, gently stroking Phantom's elegant neck.

Pixie's eyes glistened and she took another gulp of her hot chocolate, the plastic cup wobbling as she lifted it up. "I couldn't. Dad had paid for Phantom's stable, and before he left he said that he'd take care of the bills. But then Sasha told me that my next payment was overdue and Mrs Compton couldn't get hold of Dad. She said I ought to start looking for somewhere else for Phantom if he didn't cough up some more money soon." Pixie looked at the floor. "Only, I knew that would be pretty unlikely."

"Why?" Mia asked gently.

"Because I haven't heard from Dad since he left," she said, sniffing quietly and wiping her nose on her sleeve. "Mum said something about him meeting a new girlfriend at his work. It's like he's forgotten all about me and Mum, back here in stuffy England and all boring. I suppose I secretly hoped that he'd remember about the livery fees and sort it all out with Mrs Compton, but he didn't. I tried to tell Mum about it, but she hates talking about him, said we didn't need him anyway and that was the end of it. I didn't want to keep upsetting her, so I let it drop. Then I got to Compton Manor last weekend before anyone else and found Phantom wandering about the yard. I looked at his stable door and saw that the clip had been taken off it. I guessed it was one of Sasha's so-called pranks. I was about to lead him back into his stable, when I had an idea – if I moved quickly I could pretend that Phantom had just strayed from the yard and got lost. I grabbed a few bits and I just led him out and did the only thing I could think of…"

"Hid him at the Old Forge," Mia said, frowning.

"I know it was bad, but I couldn't think what else to do," Pixie explained desperately. "And Phantom's always had this unusual neigh – not like a proper one at all, more like an echo of one.

It's kind of what gave me the idea about keeping him here. I already knew about the Legend of the Old Forge, and I thought if anyone got close and heard him, well, they'd be spooked and steer clear. I thought it would mean he wouldn't get discovered."

Mia suddenly clicked. His strange neigh was probably what Mrs Millar was going to tell them about when they visited her, before she got interrupted by the phone.

"Anyway, I didn't want Mum to feel bad about Dad not paying the bills, and not being able to afford them herself. She makes jewellery, but it doesn't pay much and there's no way she'd be able to afford stabling anywhere. Or feed. So I told Mum that Phantom had gone missing."

"And *that's* why you took our pony nuts," Rosie nodded as Pixie hung her head.

"I didn't plan to," she said, going pink, "but Mum made me promise to come and see you and, well, you weren't around and I popped into the feed room for a bit to get out of the rain. I thought I'd take a few. I hadn't planned on coming back. Only, you were all so friendly and Puzzle seemed so sweet that, well... I couldn't stay away. And each time I came I ended up taking a few more pony nuts for Phantom. I'm sorry – I didn't want him to starve and I didn't know what else to do."

"It was one of those nuts that helped us solve the mystery," Rosie said. "Charlie matched one from Blackberry Farm to one at the scene. It was a vital clue which linked you to the Old Forge."

"Well, it wasn't *exactly* vital," Charlie interrupted, rolling her eyes at Rosie's exaggeration, "but finding the pony nuts did help us place you at the scene."

Pixie nodded, then explained that she'd carried bottles of water to the Forge and had snaffled some hay from Compton Manor as well as the nuts to keep Phantom going and visited him like clockwork every day after school.

"I hated lying to you all. That's why I tried

157

to say as little as possible whenever you asked me anything. I'll have to sell Phantom now I suppose," she sighed, "but it's a muddle in my head, just like you said it was with Pirate, Charlie. You'll do anything you can to hold onto him because he means the world to you, even if that means you have to give up riding. That's kind of the same as me and Phantom. I can't sell him, because he's all I've got left of Dad. But he scares me to death so there's no way I can ride him and anyway, I can't afford to keep him. I just don't know what to do."

"Er, hang on a sec," Rosie said once Pixie had finished. "Sorry, but did I just hear that you were thinking about giving up riding, Charlie?"

The three girls stared at her, open-mouthed.

Charlie shrugged miserably.

"I can't afford to buy another horse," she explained, stroking Phantom's neck absently. "Not without selling Pirate."

"But you're the best rider out of all of us put

together!" Alice said. "You can't just give up like that!

"Alice is right," Rosie added indignantly. "Ponies need you!"

Everyone sat quietly for a moment, reeling from everything Pixie had told them, not to mention the revelation that Charlie was seriously considering giving up riding after she outgrew Pirate, which was going to be very soon.

"Well, we can't stay here all night," Mia eventually said. "We'd better get back to Blackberry Farm."

Pixie looked up, anxiously.

"Don't worry," Alice said, smiling at her reassuringly. "There's one more spare stable there."

"And it's got Phantom's name on it," Rosie added. "Come on, let's get these ponies home."

Chapter Twelve

PIXIE hid her bike in the Forge, after Alice told her that her mum could drop her back home. Pixie thanked her, then uncovered the tack that she'd hidden.

"I went back to collect it last Sunday and brought it here," Pixie explained, "but there's no way I'm riding Phantom back."

"Well, I guess I could?" Charlie suggested warily, looking round at the others who all made it clear that they were with Pixie on this one. "You could ride Pirate if you like."

"My hat's at Blackberry Farm," Pixie replied quickly, looking relieved to have an excuse not to ride Charlie's spirited little bay. "But I could lead Pirate back if you don't mind riding Phantom?"

Pixie was too scared to even help tack Phantom up, and the girls quickly realised why. The black horse backed away as Charlie tried to put on his bridle, then when she finally managed to, he restlessly paced the stable as she attempted to put on his saddle and do up his girth. She was pretty worn out by the time she'd finished and they hadn't even left the stable.

"Steady boy," she whispered as she drew back the loose bolt. Phantom charged out, skidding and almost squashing Charlie, who only just managed to hold onto him. Then, as he followed the other ponies out through the creaky door, he exploded into life, plunging forward and half-rearing.

"I think it'll be safer if I just lead him home," Charlie said through gritted teeth as the reins got pulled painfully through her gloved fingers. "I don't think riding him after he's been cooped up in here for a week is such a good idea after all."

Mia stood Wish as close to Phantom as possible

to calm him, while Alice tried to get the purple rug back on over the tack, to keep the black horse warm on his walk home. He pawed the ground, lifting his fine-boned leg high and smashing his hoof on the cobbles. It just missed Charlie's foot. She felt her hands start to shake and took a deep breath as they set off. She hung onto the reins with both hands, struggling to hold Phantom as he twisted and bucked and squealed with every fresh swirl of cold wind and rain. Mia tried to keep Wish close, but she was worried about the mare being kicked or struck into. The others stayed at a safe distance, with Pixie leading a jogging Pirate and looking on in fearful awe.

"I think we should avoid any lanes," Alice called out, taking them down another bridleway to avoid stepping onto a small, windy road. But it led to an open, windswept field which ended up being just as hair-raising. Phantom plunged forward, skittish as the wind blew under his tail. He looked huge prancing along and shaking his head, spooking at every leaf that was blown up and starting at every rustle in the bushes.

"My arm is *so* stretched!" Charlie groaned, clinging onto Phantom. As Blackberry Farm finally appeared through the dusk she was seriously relieved to still have him at the end of the reins.

"Right, let's get his box ready," Mia said, as the other four raced around putting their ponies away, untacking them and rugging them up. Then they quickly cleared all the mucking-out tools and wheelbarrows from the last spare stable, swept it out and laid a deep, fresh straw bed, then filled a haynet and a water bucket.

Phantom sniffed the stable suspiciously, then rushed in. Finally, exhausted after all their stable chores, the girls got ready to leave the yard.

"Thanks so much for leading him back, Charlie," Pixie said, coming over to where Charlie was standing leaning over Phantom's stable door. "You handled him brilliantly."

"Thanks." Charlie smiled, feeling worn out but strangely captivated by the black horse, who was lingering in the shadows of his box. "I bet he's awesome to ride."

"Terrifying more like," Rosie chipped in.

"He terrified me all right, but I've never seen anyone else try," Pixie sighed, "so I've got no idea how good he is. I'd love to know, though."

She looked up at Charlie. Charlie noticed that the others were staring at her too.

"Is anyone else thinking what I'm thinking?" Pixie said, starting to smile.

Charlie looked round. Everyone was nodding and she broke into a grin.

"Looks like I'd better bring my back protector tomorrow in that case," Charlie laughed, spooking Phantom, who tossed his head in the depths of his box.

∪ ∪ ∪ ∪

The next evening, after school, Charlie noticed her fingers were shaking slightly as she tried to do up the buckle of Phantom's noseband. The black horse was electric beside her, an awesome dark force. He was standing still as she worked around him but she was aware of his sense of power, aware that she didn't know what he was thinking, as if they were a million miles apart even though she was there, standing next to him. She patted his silken neck and he tossed his head, irritably. She felt butterflies flutter as she opened the stable door and led the tall, commanding black horse out of his stable, feeling nervous about riding for the first time since she could remember.

As soon as Charlie swung her leg over the saddle it was obvious that Phantom had star quality. He was so much taller than Pirate, his neck stretching out in front of her and his withers narrow in front of the saddle. He immediately walked forward, head up, ears flashing backwards and forwards as he felt his new rider. His stride was all power but still light, and was enormous compared to Pirate's choppy pony-sized one.

"There is no way I'd get on him," Rosie whispered to Pixie. Alice and Daisy nodded vigorously in agreement as he strode past. "I don't blame you for being scared!"

They ran along ahead of Charlie as she lifted one leg in front of the saddle and tightened Phantom's girth. He started to jog, pulling at the bit anxiously. Pixie held her breath, but Charlie just sat quietly with a long rein while he danced about beneath her on the way to the paddock.

"Just start off at trot once you get here," Mrs Millar called from the middle of the ring. "He's too hot to keep at walk, and we need to get him working."

Mia had called Mrs Millar as soon as they'd found Phantom, and again later to ask her to be there while Charlie first rode him. Charlie knew that calling Mrs Millar had been the right thing to do, especially when Phantom started to put his weight into his haunches and half-rear before she'd even reached the schooling paddock.

Charlie felt herself tense. She was used to Pirate going up a bit when he was really excited, but this was something else. She swallowed hard, determined not to be scared by him. As Pixie watched Charlie, she gripped Daisy's arm, almost as nervous as if she were back on top of Phantom herself.

"Get him moving forward, Charlie, nice soft hands," Mrs Millar called out. "He's just a bit unsure, that's all."

Charlie put her legs gently on Phantom's sides, keeping her hands soft as soon as he came back down. For a moment he cantered beneath her at a walking pace, still with no weight on the reins. Charlie sat quietly with her legs still touching his sides and patted his neck. Finally, he plunged forward and started to cover some ground.

Charlie brought him quietly back to trot then put him through his paces. He fought her to start off with, bucking a couple of times and slowing right up, and threatening to rear when she asked him to do something that he didn't like, but as Mrs Millar gave them a lesson, they both started to settle. The others watched through the drizzle, captivated, as Phantom transformed in front of them with Mrs Millar's expert tuition and Charlie's skill, and they saw flashes of a beautiful, rounded trot and a stunningly smooth canter. Charlie couldn't help grinning as she circled Phantom and brought him to a halt.

"Let's try him over a fence," Mrs Millar said, directing the girls, who leaped down at once and ran to set up a place pole and a single cross pole. "Bring him in trot, Charlie."

Charlie shortened her stirrups, feeling a rush of excitement. She kept Phantom on a light rein and, in an even, bouncy trot, turned him towards the fence. He saw it, pricked his ears and rushed, but slowed for the pole and dipped his head and neck low, really arcing from his ears all the way to his tail and ballooning over the cross pole. Charlie almost laughed – she couldn't believe the feeling she'd just had. Pirate was such a good jumper and would fly over anything, but he jumped flat. Charlie had never felt a horse that jumped so cleanly and cleared the poles so effortlessly.

Mrs Millar put up another fence in the school. Phantom fought Charlie for his head on the approaches but rounded over each fence easily when he got there, tucking up his hooves neatly and clearing them cleanly. Charlie crouched lightly on top of him, her soft hands following his movement.

The watching girls held their breath as Charlie and Phantom popped over the fences. Phantom was awesome. When she pulled up, Charlie patted the black horse. He shook his head, irritated by the fuss.

"He needs plenty of work," Mrs Millar boomed, finding a mint for him which he ignored. "Got to keep his mind occupied. Lots of changes of rein, changes of pace, circles. Mix it up."

Pixie sat on the fence, looking transfixed, understanding for the first time how good her horse really was.

"I think you should try him in the Compton Manor competition, Charlie," Mrs Millar said with a smile. Pixie had filled Mrs Millar in on what life had been like at Compton Manor and Mrs Millar was keen to go there and see it for herself. She wanted a word with Mrs Compton, too, after her failure to make sure that Pixie got the help and support which had been promised. "Let you experience what he's capable of."

"You really think so?" Charlie asked, jumping off and loosening Phantom's girth, dodging his teeth as he turned to nip her, his ears back. It was Tuesday and the show was being held on Saturday. That didn't give her long to get to know Phantom.

"With the owner's permission, that is," Mrs Millar laughed, slapping Pixie on the back as they took Phantom to his stable and went to fill in the Compton Manor entry forms.

Chapter Thirteen

MRS Millar popped over to Blackberry Farm after school for the next three days to give Phantom lessons. He looked amazing, powerfully striding along under her watchful eye.

The others always watched from the fence, oohing in unison every time he put in another huge buck.

"His back hooves are *literally* going higher than your head, Charlie!" Rosie called out one time, only to be silenced with a single stare from Mrs Millar. Charlie just managed to sit to each buck, staying in the saddle as she worked to keep Phantom's head up. She reminded herself over and over to keep breathing. It felt as if Phantom was picking up on the slightest bit of tension in

Charlie, so she had to make an effort to stay relaxed. It was so strange – riding with Pirate was something she did without trying, because she and her pony knew each other so well. Now she had to think about everything for the first time in ages, and it felt exhausting.

On the first evening after Phantom had been put away, Mrs Millar had told the others that she'd give them all a lesson, and Charlie a second one, this time on Pirate. Charlie had suggested that Pixie try him, but she'd said no way. Puzzle was the only kind of pony she'd want to ride from then on. Even though for a fleeting second Charlie had hoped it would be the perfect solution, she knew deep down it wasn't right – Pirate wasn't the pony for Pixie, so Charlie didn't press it.

Knowing that Pixie's confidence had been shattered by the lethal combination of Sasha and Phantom, Mrs Millar concentrated most on Pixie and Puzzle during the lessons. Within a couple of days of Mrs Millar's teaching, Pixie was starting to believe in herself again and was riding Puzzle brilliantly.

"You're clearly a good, sympathetic rider," Mrs Millar announced as Pixie patted the blue roan. "Anyone can see that, and if someone says differently then they can't be a horseman in my book."

Pixie smiled, her cheeks glowing pink at the praise.

Daisy came along each day too, joining in the lessons as they swapped ponies, so that they all got to be taught by Mrs Millar ahead of the show. Everyone had insisted, as they untacked and stood about the yard after the final lesson on Friday, that Daisy should come with them to Compton Manor because she'd become part of the team.

"After all," Rosie pointed out, "Puzzle wouldn't be going anywhere if it wasn't for your care."

"Okay – I'll ask Hope Farm for the morning off," she finally agreed, "but I'll only go as veterinary consultant and holder of ponies. My competing days are over!"

Everyone cheered, and Alice said that Daisy could hack Scout over to Compton Manor. Alice was shorter than Charlie and she could ride Pirate instead. Charlie had decided to enter him in the 80cm class.

"Good for you," Mrs Millar nodded approvingly. "It'll be the last time you get to compete on Pirate, so you might as well make the most of it."

"Oh, yes, I hadn't thought of it like that," Charlie lied, trying to smile, but with Mrs Millar's words the stone cold, hard reality of the situation hit her. She turned back to Pirate's stable, suddenly remembering that she'd forgotten to give him the mint in her pocket.

⌣ ⌣ ⌣ ⌣

"Oh, Sasha, look!" Jade shrieked as the six girls

rode into Compton Manor on Saturday morning. There were loads of people and ponies milling about but worse luck, they had bumped straight into the CM club. "The entertainment's turned up, and it looks like she's riding some kind of scruffy cob – what a comedown from Phantom!"

Pixie went bright red and patted Puzzle's roan neck, while Daisy told her to ignore them. Pixie had spent ages with Daisy, grooming Puzzle until he was beautifully clean. They'd even plaited his mane and tail, which Pixie had loved doing. According to Mia, who didn't often give praise for grooming, she had a real talent for turnout, only now Pixie was back at Compton Manor, she looked as if she wished she could disappear again.

"And there's Phantom!" Alice heard Bex say, sounding relieved and earning a scowl from Sasha, who turned round and scrutinised the black horse. He looked a million dollars, but Sasha wasn't impressed, or at least didn't show it if she was.

"I wouldn't enter that horse into any of our classes if I were you," she sneered. "He hates the indoor school here."

"Something to do with the loudspeaker used to make the announcements," Jade laughed. "We tried to get him used to it by talking in it while Pixie was schooling, but I think we may have made him worse – shame."

Charlie scowled at them and patted Phantom's taut neck. She noticed that, although he'd jig-jogged and pulled on the reins on the ride over, reminding her of a larger version of Pirate, he'd been fairly settled. But now he was among all the other ponies and standing still he was starting to get on his toes again, snorting and growing taller by the second.

"Which class are you in, anyway?" Sasha asked as Mrs Millar came over and gave Phantom a pat, before checking his girth.

"The Junior Trophy," Charlie replied.

"You're up against Sasha," Jade jeered, before

bursting into laughter, nudging Bex to do the same. Bex frowned, then pretended to smile when she saw Sasha glaring at her. Sasha looked smug before opening her stable door and leading The Colonel out.

"I'll see you in the ring, then," she replied coolly, "and may the best rider win."

As Sasha rode off to the warm-up area, Mrs Millar organised everyone for their classes, getting numbers for those that needed them before helping Pixie and Puzzle prepare for the clear round competition, where they'd be jumping a small course of fences with the promise of a rosette if they kept all the poles up.

When Pixie was ready, they all rode round to the indoor school. It was huge, with mirrors all down each side, making it seem even bigger. The surface was a deep brown, even and immaculately maintained. High up to the side was a gallery, with seats rising row by row. It was packed. One end of the school had post-and-rail fencing and a gate, where the competitors rode in and out. Anyone could stand at that end and watch what was happening inside and still keep hold of their ponies. Charlie jumped off Phantom, and passed his reins to Mrs Millar so that she could take Pirate. They all gathered by the gate to watch as Pixie rode into the school, pale and twitchy.

The course was small and rode well, with lots of space between fences. Pixie gathered her reins and popped Puzzle into a steady canter. She looked for each fence in turn and told Puzzle how good he was each time he cleared a jump.

"Pixie and Puzzle jump clear!" the loudspeaker announced, as Pixie collected a rosette on her way out.

"That's the first rosette I've *ever* won!" She beamed, looking almost as if she might cry she was so happy, lying along the pony's neck and patting him with both hands as Daisy found him some mints. "Puzzle, you're a complete star!"

It was the start of a good run. Rosie and Mia

both managed clears at the first attempt and Rosie even looked half decent after Mrs Millar's last minute tuition. But in the 80cm competition Alice was eliminated after she got distracted by the audience in the gallery and missed out a fence. Charlie followed her in on Pirate and he flew round, rattling each fence but leaving them all standing, earning himself a place in the jump-off. Charlie took her pony outside and walked him round while the other ponies jumped the shortened course against the clock. She was last to go, and when the second to last pony rode out of the arena, Charlie jogged Pirate back in, one hand on his neck. Suddenly it hit her, full force: this would be the last time the pair would compete together.

"This is it, Pirate," she whispered, patting his sturdy neck beneath the thick black mane as her pony bunny-hopped, eager to go. For a second she felt her heart quiver, then she smiled, feeling a warm buzz of love and determination race through her. "So let's make this a good one."

She leaned forward a fraction as the bell went, and Pirate immediately took it as his signal to go. Charlie focused as she asked Pirate for breathtaking turns, twisting between fences as he choppily dodged and jumped, spun and flew. Charlie heard the crowd gasp, watching the impossible line she was taking. But she knew Pirate, and the more challenges she set him, the braver he got. And she knew, as they flew through the finishing line, Pirate's ears still pricked, that he'd loved every second as much as she had. They'd rattled fences, but left every one up, and easily clocked the fastest time. He was flying so fast that it took her a whole circuit to pull him up.

After she brought him back to a halt, they waited to collect the small cup and rosette. Charlie beamed and patted Pirate's neck. She wished she could freeze time right there, forever, that she could stop growing and carry on riding Pirate always. But she knew she was desperately wishing for the impossible. Especially when she heard the loudspeaker crackle into life.

"The next class is the Junior Trophy for the Under 16s," the loudspeaker announced.

Charlie closed her eyes for a second, blinking them hard as she leaned forward and gave Pirate a hug. With a final squeeze she sat back up and rode out of the ring, her eyes glistening. She jumped down and passed her little bay's reins, his cup and rosette to Alice.

"Perfect round," Alice said, as Mia and Rosie smiled. They could all guess how Charlie must be feeling as she patted Pirate. For a second Charlie couldn't speak, looking at the tiny little Pirate, standing so alertly, so eager to please and such a willing partner in everything they'd done. She took a deep breath and smiled.

"Totally perfect," she agreed. She knew it couldn't have been better. But she didn't have long to think about it, because Sasha marched past to organise the jumps for the trophy and Charlie knew that she had to get Phantom ready.

Sasha ordered the Under 16s of the yard, including Tom, Jade and Bex, around the ring, directing where to put up fences and walking between them with her measuring wheel. She was making a big deal of checking her plan, then striding out the related distances in the doubles and combinations to ensure that they were right. Once it was complete, Mia took hold of Phantom and Charlie found Mrs Millar to walk the course.

Sasha was just ahead of them with Jade, giggling the whole way and looking round at everyone else, being really annoying. Mrs Millar strode it out with Charlie and they emerged looking serious.

"It's going to be a testing course for this horse," Mrs Millar said as she legged Charlie back into the saddle. "Those combinations are all extremely short."

They all looked at Phantom, who was long in the back. It couldn't be less ideal for him and it was going to test Charlie's skills to the max. She felt herself shiver.

"It's almost as if the course has been designed to suit a very short-striding horse," Mrs Millar said grimly as they watched Sasha and The Colonel, who was sweating after being ridden in for ages, canter into the ring, first to go. The Colonel bounced neatly over one fence then another, finding all the distances perfect. Mrs Millar frowned. "Not unlike that one in the ring right now…"

"You jumped that brilliantly!" Jade exclaimed, trying not to laugh as Sasha cleared the last fence and rode out. "Almost as if the course was built just for you!"

Sasha smiled knowingly before jumping off and throwing her reins at Bex, who looked at The Colonel with concern. "Do you want me to walk him round at all, until he's cooled down?"

"No. Just tie him up until it's time to collect the Trophy," she crowed. "It won't be long. After all, there won't be any others in the jump-off, not over *this* course!"

As the Pony Detectives looked on, Tom's cremello pony, Casper, refused the last fence in the combination and they ended up being eliminated. Others fared no better, with rider after rider getting into trouble with the short distances between fences, knocking poles down left, right and centre. The way the class was going it would be almost impossible for anyone else to go clear. Sasha would win with a course that looked more and more as if it had been designed and built by Sasha to suit The Colonel.

Charlie tried to put that out of her mind as she trotted Phantom around the warm-up arena, riding the course in her head and repeating all Mrs Millar's advice to herself. She breathed out, telling herself that it was only a show and it didn't matter how they did. But secretly, deep down, she felt worried on top of a horse for the first time ever, not knowing what might happen as she rode out of the practice ring, past the others and into the main arena.

She could tell that Phantom was on edge as soon as he'd walked through the huge doors into the indoor school. And when the loudspeaker crackled to announce that Faraway Phantom and Charlotte Hall were in the ring, he jinked backwards, his ears flat. Charlie patted him and managed to keep him contained until the bell went and he half-reared. He came back to the ground and immediately did it again, swinging round at the same time.

"I bet he remembers Sasha scaring him in there," Pixie whispered to Alice and Mrs Millar, looking panicked as Phantom started to back up.

But Charlie didn't give up. She suddenly realised that he was more scared than she was, and he needed her to be confident and brave for his sake. She relaxed in the saddle and, rather than hurrying Phantom, she sat quietly, waiting for him to calm down. She could sense that he wasn't being naughty. As Charlie sat with soft hands, not putting any pressure on him, he suddenly stopped and stood quietly for a moment. Then Charlie put her legs on gently and together the pair of them set off with a bound. Pixie and Alice both let out a big sigh of relief.

Charlie stuck to the exact route that she'd walked with Mrs Millar. Phantom fought the bit, lifting his head up, but stayed light in his mouth and arced over the first few fences when he reached them. Charlie could feel that Phantom was clearing each fence by masses and felt a buzz of excitement, until they got to the first double, where his scope would be likely to land him in trouble if he jumped in big. Charlie held Phantom together, getting him right back on his hocks going into the first fence and then again as she landed, then Phantom popped over the second fence, a big parallel, clearing it easily. Charlie stroked his neck briefly and flicked his ears back, listening to her.

They easily cleared the next couple of jumps,

then turned to the combination. It was a parallel, followed by an upright, followed by a huge triple bar, with one stride between the first two fences and two strides between the last two. The whole gallery fell silent. Charlie knew that if she went in too slow Phantom wouldn't make the back bars of the fences; too fast, and she'd crash straight into the second fence like so many of the other riders in the class.

Charlie steadied Phantom, who shook his head, in the final few strides but she kept her legs on to maintain the impulsion and he jumped in big over the parallel. The back pole rocked as Charlie held Phantom together, snapping back in the saddle so that he didn't run on to the middle fence. She held him for the single stride, just letting him jump out of her hands over the upright, which he cleared on a bouncy stride. But he landed further out than Charlie would have liked with his floaty jump. Now, with only a stride and a half between them and the next fence, they were in trouble.

But rather than sit and try for the two strides, Charlie instinctively squeezed him up, her reins soft. Phantom responded in an instant and stretched out, taking one massive, raking stride before launching himself skyward and powering up over the triple bar. He snapped his hooves up to keep them out of the way of the poles. They soared over it, landing softly on the other side.

Pixie and Alice burst out cheering as they watched them clear the rest of the course, flying over the last fence easily. Phantom bucked twice before Charlie brought him back to a walk. She broke into a smile, relief washing over her. Then suddenly she got excited about what they'd just done together. In the end, they'd made a tricky course look simple.

Sasha's face was thunderous when Charlie rode out, patting Phantom happily as he jogged his head up and down, white foam flicking from his bit. It was time for the jump-off. And it soon became very obvious that Sasha had been so convinced that she'd be the only clear that she hadn't bothered thinking about the second course. She snapped at Jade and Bex as they got a harassed-looking Colonel ready for Sasha to warm up. She was going first, and after a couple of jumps in the practice ring she cantered him into the arena.

In the silence, she messed up the approach to nearly every fence. The Colonel swished his tail, getting confused as Sasha pulled and kicked, until at the penultimate fence he ground to a halt in front of it, sending Sasha flying. She jumped back on, bright red, and shouted at him. He refused to budge, standing there with his heels dug in, his head high and his ears back, looking thoroughly fed up and frightened until Sasha dismounted again and left him standing in the arena. Bex ran in to rescue the chestnut as the voice over the loudspeaker announced that The Colonel and Sasha Compton had been eliminated.

"At least I know that maniac horse won't do

any better," she raged, storming out as Charlie cantered Phantom into the ring.

Charlie felt more confident going back in, but after his performance at the start of the last round Charlie wasn't sure what to expect. Phantom was more settled and only jinked once when the voice over the loudspeaker said their names.

"Come on Phantom," Charlie whispered. He flicked one ear back. "Let's show them what you can do."

Then, light as a feather, he moved smoothly from walk to canter and Charlie guided him to the first fence, keeping her legs against him and allowing her hands to go forward, following his head as it stretched down. He glided over each fence and this time the striding in the double that ended the course was easier. Phantom floated effortlessly over the first one, landing lightly and adjusting his stride to pop out over the second element of the double, the last fence in the course.

As the arena erupted into a roar, sending

Phantom into a fizzing frenzy, Charlie rode him quietly out of the arena at a sideways, slow-motion canter, his head tucked into his chest, white foam from his bit flecking his coat. Charlie had to pinch herself, suddenly realising that she'd ridden round the whole course and hadn't heard a single rap of the fences.

"That's because he cleared them all by a whole mile!" Rosie squealed as Charlie rode, breathless and beaming, out of the ring.

Apart from Jade and Sasha, everyone from the yard cheered loudly during the presentation. Sasha's mother congratulated Charlie warmly on her riding when she handed her the prize, saying that she must have another look at Sasha's course design; she was sure she hadn't approved quite such a stiff test for the juniors.

As they left the arena Mrs Millar disappeared to have a word with Mrs Compton and the girls saw Sasha blaming Bex for The Colonel's poor performance.

"You must have upset him when you tied him in his stable," Sasha shouted. "I told you to walk him round! It's all your fault!"

"Well, if you'd have looked after your poor horse yourself then you wouldn't have anyone else to blame, would you?" Bex suddenly shouted back, astonishing Sasha, who stood there open-mouthed and unable to reply.

They watched as Bex then strode straight up to an already flustered-looking Mrs Compton and handed her two pieces of paper with the course drawn on.

As Bex walked away with her head held high, Sasha blurted out that she was out of the CM club for good.

"Don't worry," Bex said triumphantly. "It's not just the CM club I'm out of. It's Compton Manor too – I'm going to move my pony to a new yard as soon as I can find a box. There's no way I'm staying in this place for a minute longer while you're in charge of the Under 16s!"

"Well said!" Tom laughed, joining forces. "And I'll be following you, Bex."

As others from the Junior yard joined in, the Pony Detectives heard a voice calling out, sounding furious.

"Sasha!" Mrs Compton, almost purple and furiously waving the two bits of paper Bex had given her, came stomping up the yard. "You're in serious trouble!"

Chapter Fourteen

MRS Millar had driven away from the show, calling Charlie and Phantom a 'perfect match', and saying that she should seriously consider making it a permanent partnership. Charlie had been floating on cloud nine, but her mood had quickly dropped as reality set in on the ride back to Blackberry Farm.

"If you *did* buy him," Daisy said excitedly, "Pixie could see him all the time even though she didn't own him."

Pixie looked reluctant and Charlie shook her head. "There's no way Mum and Dad could afford to buy Phantom," she explained.

"Hang on," Mia said suddenly having a bright idea. "There is one possible way! What if Charlie took Phantom on loan? That way you still get to ride without having to sell Pirate, and Pixie still officially owns Phantom?"

"Perfect!" Alice and Rosie grinned.

Charlie looked at Pixie questioningly. Pixie frowned, then smiled. "That might just work!"

"I'd have to check with my parents first, though, about keeping two ponies," Charlie said, feeling the excitement start to bubble up inside her again, even though she wasn't sure what her parents would say. "I'll give them a ring as soon as we get back!"

"And no one's claimed Puzzle, yet," Rosie said to Pixie as everyone else nodded, "so it makes sense for you to keep looking after him."

"Could you imagine it!" Pixie breathed. "Puzzle's my dream pony, and I know I shouldn't have, but I've completely fallen in love with him!"

Pixie wanted to say more, but something inside her couldn't quite believe that things could turn out so magically well, and she didn't dare jinx it.

As soon as they got back to Blackberry Farm, Charlie called her parents, but they weren't in, so she left them a garbled, excited message.

Daisy helped untack, then sighed. "I've had the best day ever," she said, "but I've got to leave so I can check on Rolo. I'll see you all tomorrow afternoon."

She patted Puzzle once more, then disappeared on her bike, leaving the ponies noisily eating from their haynets. The others gathered in the hay barn. They rested Phantom's silver trophy on one of the bales and toasted his and Charlie's success with a chink of hot chocolate mugs.

"You know what this means, don't you Pixie?" Mia said, suddenly turning very serious. "Your name gets called out at every show as the owner of Phantom – you're the owner of your very own competition horse!"

"You'll have to attend every show Charlie goes to," Rosie added, as Charlie smiled, getting excited too. Pixie giggled, going pink, her eyes wide as she thought about what lay ahead.

"Then when everyone starts raving about him," Alice beamed, "which they will, you can say, 'That's *my* horse you're talking about!'"

Pixie laughed, almost falling off the hay bale and making the others start to giggle too. Only Mia noticed Mrs Honeycott hurrying into the barn, carrying a cordless phone. As the others carried on laughing, Mia went to the top of the ladder.

"Phonecall for the Pony Detectives," Mrs Honeycott called, as she handed the phone up to Mia. "I couldn't quite make out who it was."

Mia's smile faded at once. There was only one person who would call the Blackberry Farm number and ask for the Pony Detectives. Mia held the phone to her ear, feeling her hand shake slightly.

"Hello?" she said, as she sank back down onto the hay bales, next to the others.

Everyone gradually fell silent as Mia started

talking to the person at the other end of the phone. Even though they could only hear one side of the conversation it was clear what it was about. Pixie held her breath, looking pale.

"Yes, just past the post box, then it's second on the right," Mia explained quietly. "We'll have him ready."

Mia looked up at Pixie after the call ended. They all knew what was coming.

"That was Puzzle's owner," Mia said. "The field where we put up the note was his, after all."

"It's all right, really. I mean, it was always going to happen wasn't it?" Pixie said, trying to smile as if everything was okay, as if she was always used to things not working out for her. But she couldn't pretend for long and she suddenly turned and rushed down the ladder. As they looked out of the cracks in the barn they saw her fly across the yard to Puzzle's stable.

"I'd better let Daisy know," Mia said, starting to text.

The next fifteen minutes whizzed by. Charlie's phone finally rang and she ducked into Pirate's stable to answer it just as Beanie started barking, rushing to the gate as he heard a car pull into the drive. Pixie stood with Puzzle, red-eyed but looking resigned. She'd undone all the roan pony's plaits which had made his mane go wavy. His clear round rosette was still tied outside his stable.

"I want his owner to see that Puzzle's been well looked after," she whispered, not looking at Alice while she stroked his neck over and over.

Mia walked to the gate as a car pulling an old trailer slowed to a halt. An elderly lady climbed slowly out of the passenger seat and a tall girl jumped out from the driver's side and suddenly brightened.

"Ghost!" she called out.

The blue roan pony raised his head and whickered softly, his ears pricked. The girl ran across and Pixie let herself out of the stable, standing to one side as the girl hugged him and gave him a couple of carrots from her pocket. The elderly woman followed her through the gate using a stick to walk with.

After the girl had finished giving Puzzle – or Ghost as they now knew his real name was – lots of fuss, they all went into the tack room. Charlie let herself out of Pirate's stable and joined them, sitting next to Alice on a blanket box. Alice noticed her hands shaking slightly.

"Did you speak to your parents?" Alice asked in a whisper. Charlie nodded. "Everything okay?" Charlie looked up and saw Pixie standing dejectedly in the door way. "Tell you later," Charlie whispered back, and sat fiddling with Pirate's headcollar.

"I'm so glad Ghost found you kind girls," the elderly woman remarked once Mia had explained what had happened. "I've been trying to look after him for my granddaughter Abby here since she went to university a month ago, and it's proved a bit beyond me."

The girl next to her smiled sadly. "Nan said she'd keep an eye out for him. Only now I can see that wasn't fair. On either of them."

"It was fine to begin with," the old woman said, patting Abby's knee lightly as she went on, and gesturing at her stick. "I gave him hay, had the farrier out and checked on him every day. Until a couple of weeks ago. I had a bad fall and had to go into hospital. I hoped Ghost might be all right as long as he had some grass to eat – I didn't want Abby to worry or miss any of her studies, so I didn't say anything to her. Then I found your note yesterday when I got back and I felt terrible about the poor pony. I called Abby straight away. She left first thing this morning. As soon as she arrived, we called you."

"What we really need," Abby said looking round hopefully, "is for someone to take him on permanent loan, someone who wouldn't mind me turning up every now and again in the holidays to have a few rides."

"Did you hear that, Pixie?" Rosie grinned, turning to look at her. But the doorway was empty and there was only the sound of footsteps running through the yard. The girls exchanged puzzled looks, then ran after her. She was sitting in the barn, her arms wrapped around her knees, her chin resting on them miserably.

"Pixie? Did you hear what Abby said?" Mia asked, frowning.

"She's looking for someone to take Puzzle on loan. Full time!" Rosie added excitedly.

"It's perfect," Alice said. "Charlie looks after Phantom and you loan Puzzle. It works out all round, just like we planned, right Charlie?"

Charlie nodded, scuffing the hay with her foot. Pixie looked up desperately, her eyes shining and tears streaking her pale face.

"But it's not perfect, is it?" Pixie said sadly, shaking her head. "That was just a lovely day dream. I couldn't afford Phantom. I can't afford Puzzle… I mean Ghost. I can't afford to keep him or stable him or… or look after him properly. He'd end up in another field just like the one he escaped from."

They all stood for a second, not quite knowing what to say.

"I'm sorry Charlie," Pixie sniffed. "I feel like I've ruined everything."

"You haven't," Charlie said, trying to smile. "I guess we all just got carried away."

Mia frowned, then reached for her mobile phone and left the barn quietly.

"I'd better go and tell Abby and her nan," Charlie said, slipping after Mia.

A few moments later Pixie, Alice and Rosie heard a bolt being drawn back and a clip-clop of hooves. Covering her ears, Pixie got up and ran out to the paddock at the back of the yard, her breath coming fast as her hair flopped over her face, tears dropping from her cheeks. With just one phone call all her dreams had been shattered. She couldn't help but hear an engine starting up in the distance, then the rattling of a trailer making its way slowly along the rutted drive.

"You can ride Scout any time you want to," Alice said, coming up behind with Rosie and putting her arms around Pixie's shaking shoulders.

"And Dancer," Rosie added. "Not that you'd probably want to – she's a bit of a slow coach – but you can drop by here whenever you want."

Pixie nodded with a sniff. When they heard the noise of the engine fade they walked heavily back to the yard.

Pixie looked away from Ghost's empty stable, but she couldn't help one quick glance. She stopped in her tracks. There, standing quietly just like nothing had happened, was a large blue roan pony.

"But…?" Pixie asked in a whisper. "I don't understand!"

At that moment Mia walked over, grinning, and held out her phone to Pixie. "I've got Daisy on speaker phone, she wants a word."

"Daisy?" Pixie said, confused. "What's going on?"

"Mia called me," Daisy explained excitedly down the phone, "to tell me about Puzzle needing someone to loan him. She put me onto to Abby and..."

"...and?" Pixie asked, hardly daring to listen.

"And, I told her that I've got a field shelter and an unused paddock, so would she consider loaning Ghost to me?"

Pixie's mouth dropped open. "What did she say?"

"Yes, of course!" Daisy giggled as Pixie's eyes lit up. "Dad's delighted that I want another pony, one that suits me this time and he's said he'll cover all the costs! He even suggested Abby and her Nan come over here to get everything sorted. They were about to load Ghost to take him back to his field, but they put him back in his stable instead and they're on their way to mine now, so they can see the stables and the paddock, and then we can go through a loan agreement. If everything's okay, Abby said she'll help me move Ghost later this afternoon!"

"That's excellent news!" Alice cheered.

"Well, almost, but there's still one snag," Daisy said seriously. "You see, although all the costs are covered, with the job at Hope Farm I don't have enough time to look after Ghost on my own. So I'll need someone to share him with me. Know anyone…?"

Pixie beamed, laughing out loud. Then she skipped over to tell Ghost the good news.

♩ ♩ ♩ ♩

Abby's car pulled the horse trailer slowly down Blackberry Farm's drive, with Ghost's blue roan rump just visible from the outside. Charlie stood quietly at the top of the drive, behind the other three Pony Detectives, who were all waving wildly. Daisy and Pixie leaned out of the car and waved back, almost bursting with excitement about showing Puzzle his new home. They called out goodbyes until the car and trailer had slowly bumped all the way to the end of the drive and turned the corner onto Duck Lane, disappearing from sight.

"Another case successfully completed," Rosie said, sounding satisfied. "One Phantom found, one Puzzle solved and lots of missing pony nuts accounted for."

"And one new horse for the yard, so now we have five!" Alice added as they turned towards it, the rosettes from Compton Manor pinned up against the stables, except for Ghost's rosette, which had been taken down to be transported with him to his new stable.

"Not quite," Charlie said, her voice wobbling. The others all turned towards her, frowning.

"What do you mean?"

"I... I didn't want to say anything while Pixie was here," Charlie began hesitantly. "She was so happy and I didn't want to spoil it. But I spoke to Mum and Dad..."

"And?" Mia asked.

"And," Charlie said taking a deep breath, "they've said that they're okay about me taking on Phantom, but they can't afford to keep him *and* Pirate. So, I've got to make a decision."

Charlie looked up and saw the huge red rosette fluttering from Phantom's stable door. He was standing near the back of his stable, keeping out of sight. The other four ponies all had their heads over their doors, ears pricked as they listened to the sound of the rattling trailer finally fading to nothing.

"I can either keep Pirate but give up riding," Charlie sighed, "or I can take on Phantom and lose Pirate."

"What are you going to do?" Rosie asked, feeling the tension in the air.

"Well, I know more than anyone how much Pirate loves charging round the countryside, flying over fences. He... he needs someone who'll do all that with him," she said, trying to sound matter-of-fact, until her voice trembled and gave her away. "But I won't ever sell him, he'll always belong to me and I'll always make sure he's okay and well cared for, no matter what."

Charlie looked over at Pirate's mischievous little face, his bright eyes almost hidden behind his bushy forelock. He didn't have a clue that everything was changing around him, that nothing would ever truly be the same again. Charlie walked towards him and gently pulled his soft, stubby ear. She thought of his nostrils fluttering warmly when she arrived at the yard every morning, his excitement at seeing the tack being slung over his stable door, his huge heart as brave as a lion's, no matter what fence they were facing.

"So there's only one problem left to solve now then," Alice sighed.

"Finding a new rider for Pirate," Rosie said grimly.

They gathered by Pirate's stable. They all knew that Charlie's decision was the right one, the only one she could really make. It would be the worst fate of all for Pirate to be left standing in the paddock, watching the other ponies leaving the yard to be ridden out.

"We'll all help you find the best person *ever* for him," Mia said, "The Pony Detectives are totally on the case."

Charlie nodded, unable to speak as she turned to Pirate. He nudged her arm, looking expectantly at her. Charlie's heart melted. He trusted her completely and she wouldn't let him down. The next few weeks and months would be the most heartbreaking she'd ever had to face, but with her best friends beside her, she knew they'd find a way through, together.

Turn over for some
fantastic pony tips from
The Pony Detectives
and their pals!

Daisy's First Aid Kit

Make sure you keep a pony first aid kit at the yard so you can deal with any minor cuts and scrapes. It could also help in an emergency while you wait for the vet!

Torch
A small torch will be useful if you have to check your pony in the dark.

Bowl, towel and wash
Antibacterial wash, a bowl and a towel to dry the area around a wound are all very useful. It's important that the bowl and the towel are nice and clean.

Curved scissors
You'll need round-edged scissors to trim the hair near the edges of a wound. Be really careful when you're using these!

Wound gel
Wound gel creates a protective barrier over a cut and stops bacteria or dirt from getting in.

Sterile dressings
Use sterile dressings to cover and protect an injury.

Bandages and gamgee
Gamgee are pads that go over the sterile dressing to keep it in place. Bandages go on top of the gamgee. They can help to support the injured leg.

DAISY'S STAR TIP
If there's something in a cut, or it's deep or swollen, OR if you're just not sure, always call the vet.

Gamgee

Bandage

The Pony Detectives' Introduction to Lunging

What's it all about? Lunging is great training for your pony. He will walk, trot and canter in a twenty metre circle, on the end of a lunge line.

Cavesson

What equipment do I need?
↻ A lunge line
↻ A bridle or a cavesson
↻ A lunge whip, to stop your pony wandering into the circle to see you!
↻ Brushing boots, to protect your pony's legs from knocks.

How's it done? The pony moves round in a big circle while the trainer stands in the centre, using voice commands to vary the pony's pace. The trainer changes the direction of the circle so that the pony works both sides equally.

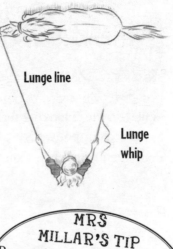

Lunge line

Lunge whip

Why do it?

1 It can be used, like Mrs Millar does, to exercise a young pony. It helps build up his muscles, ready for wearing a saddle.

MRS MILLAR'S TIP
Remember to wear gloves! If your pony gets excited and pulls the lunge line through your hands, it will hurt!

2 You can lunge an excitable pony before you ride him, so he can get rid of some of his extra energy!

3 It can help you improve your riding. An instructor will lunge the pony while you concentrate on perfecting your position in the saddle.

Rosie's Tips for Finding the Perfect Yard or School

Whether you're looking for a riding school or a yard to stable your pony, my tips will help you avoid what Pixie went through at Compton Manor!

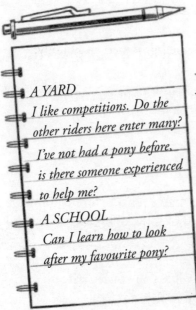

A YARD
I like competitions. Do the other riders here enter many?

I've not had a pony before. is there someone experienced to help me?

A SCHOOL
Can I learn how to look after my favourite pony?

↺ First, write a list of what you want from a yard or a school.

↺ Take your list with you when you visit all the yards and riding schools.

Other useful things to think about:

♘ When you walk in, does everyone make you feel really welcome?

♘ If you're looking for a yard, are the ponies' haynets full and their beds clean?

♘ If you're checking out a riding school, watch a couple of lessons to see what the teaching is like.

♘ Do the ponies look well-groomed and happy?

Take as much time as you can to decide, it should be perfect for you and your pony pal!